ALADDIN
and the
Magic Lamp

D0685801

STONE ARCH BOOKS
a capstone imprint

ALADDIN and the Magic Lamp

RETOLD BY **CARL BOWEN**
ILLUSTRATED BY **ALFONSO RUIZ**

DESIGNER: **BRANN GARVEY** ART DIRECTOR: **BOB LENTZ**

EDITOR: **DONALD LEMKE** CREATIVE DIRECTOR: **HEATHER KINDSETH**

ASSOC. EDITOR: **SEAN TULIEN** EDITORIAL DIRECTOR: **MICHAEL DAHL**

Published by Stone Arch Books, A Capstone Imprint 1710 Roe Crest Drive, North Mankato, Minnesota 56003 www.capstonepub.com Copyright © 2011 by Stone Arch Books All rights reserved.
No part of this publication may be reproduced in whole or in part, or stored in a retrieval system, or transmitted in any form or by any means, electronic, mechanical, photocopying, recording, or otherwise, without written permission of the publisher.

Cataloging-in-Publication Data is available on the Library of Congress website.

ISBN: 978-1-4342-1942-8 (library binding)
ISBN: 978-1-4342-2774-4 (paperback)

Summary: The story of Aladdin, a poor youth living in Al Kal'as. One day, the crafty boy outsmarts an evil sorcerer, getting his hands on a magical lamp that houses a wish-fulfilling genie! Soon, all of Aladdin's dreams come true, and he finds himself wealthy and married to a beautiful princess. All is well until, one day, the evil sorcerer returns to reclaim the magical lamp.

Printed in the United States of America in North Mankato, Minnesota.
082016
009931R

CONTENTS

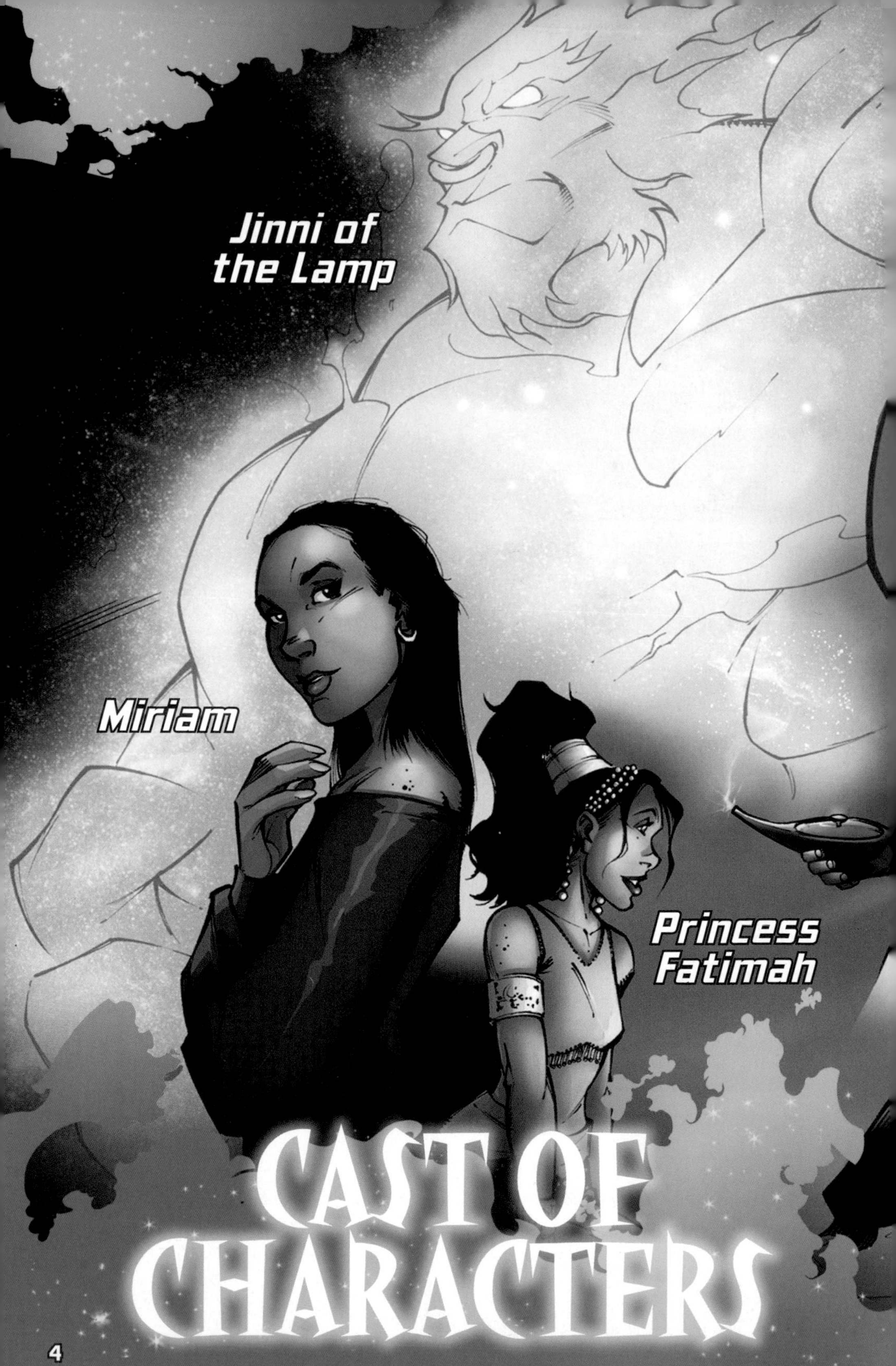
Jinni of the Lamp
Miriam
Princess Fatimah
CAST OF CHARACTERS

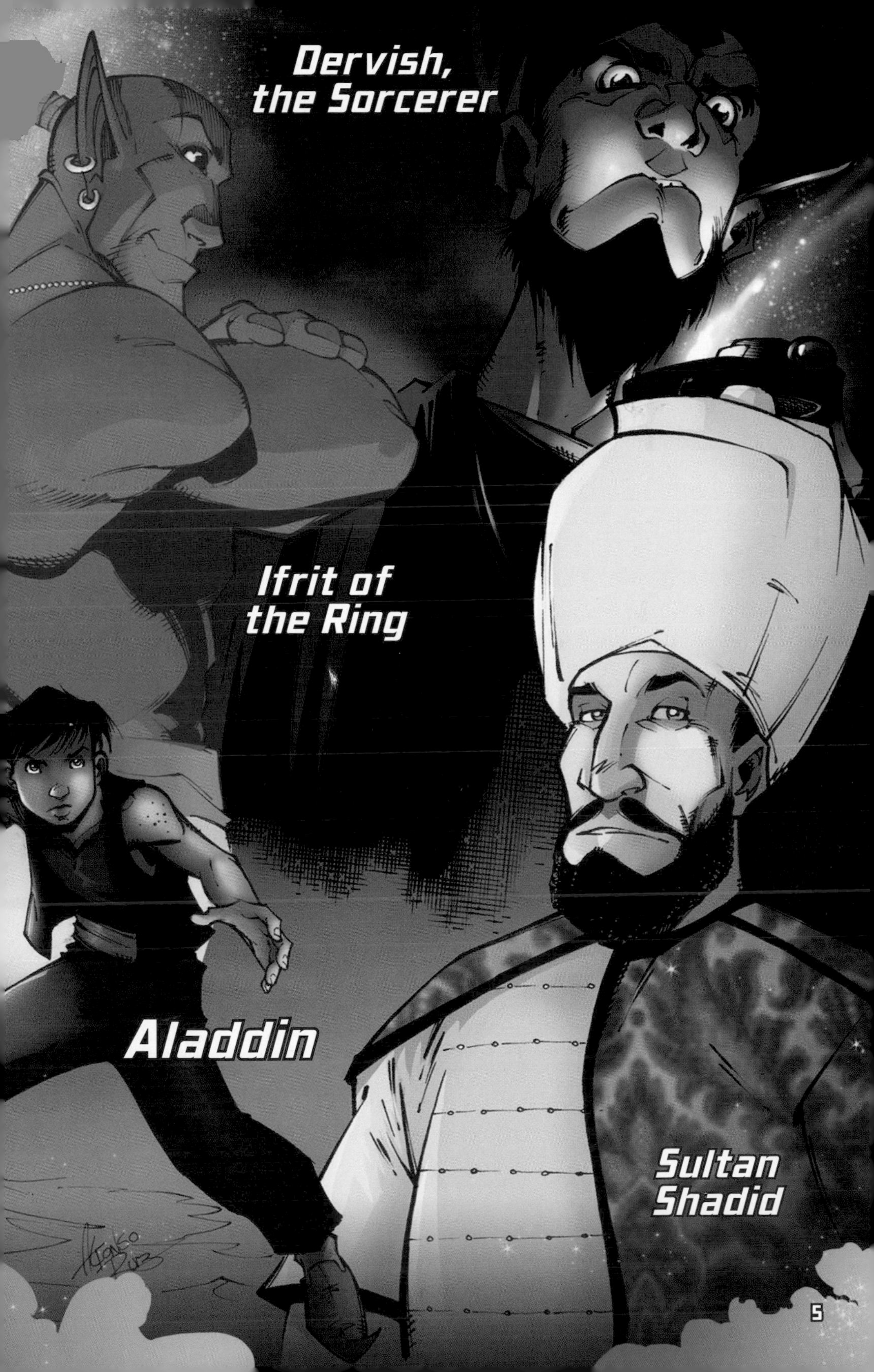
Dervish, the Sorcerer
Ifrit of the Ring
Aladdin
Sultan Shadid

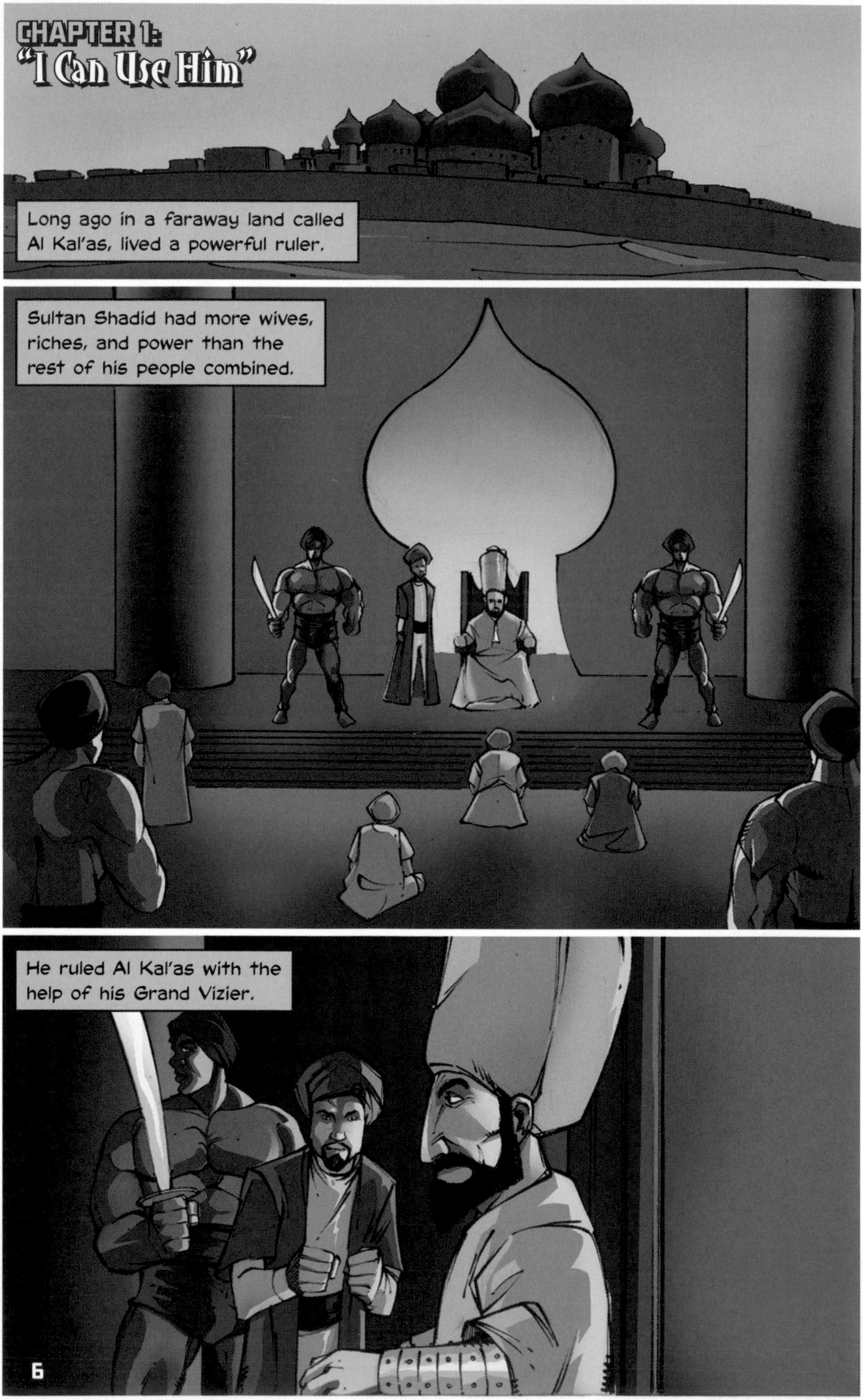
CHAPTER 1:
"I Can Use Him"
Long ago in a faraway land called Al Kal'as, lived a powerful ruler.
Sultan Shadid had more wives, riches, and power than the rest of his people combined.
He ruled Al Kal'as with the help of his Grand Vizier.

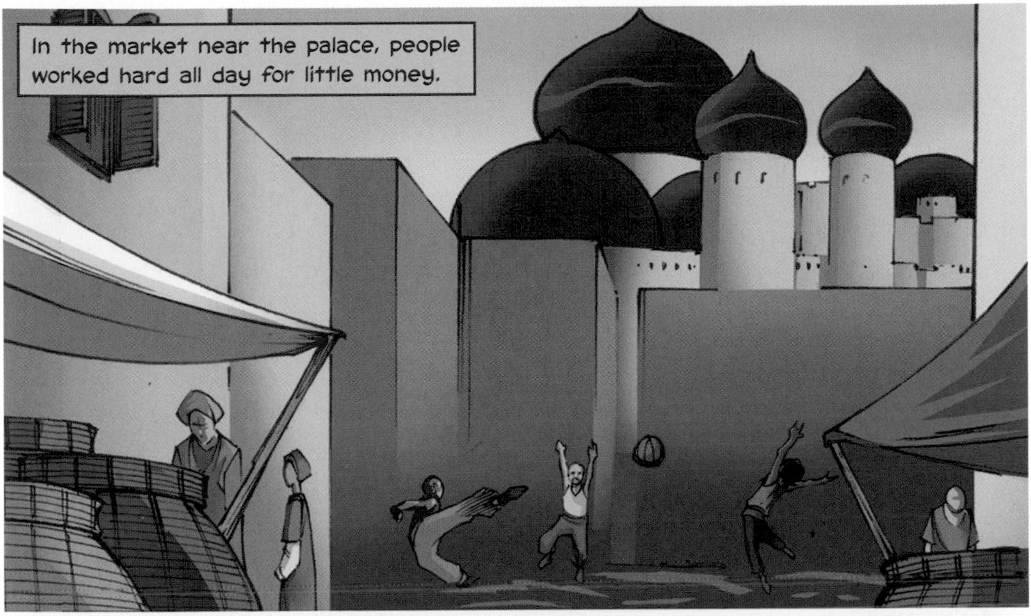
In the market near the palace, people worked hard all day for little money.

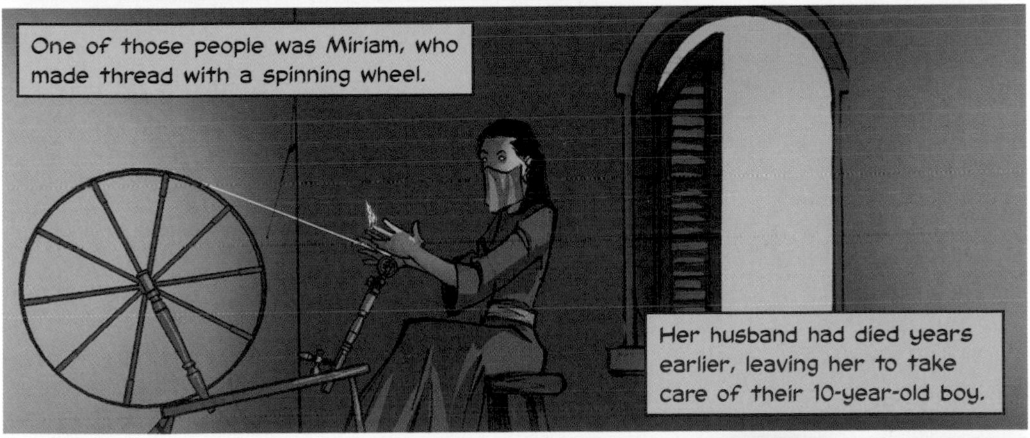
One of those people was Miriam, who made thread with a spinning wheel.
Her husband had died years earlier, leaving her to take care of their 10-year-old boy.

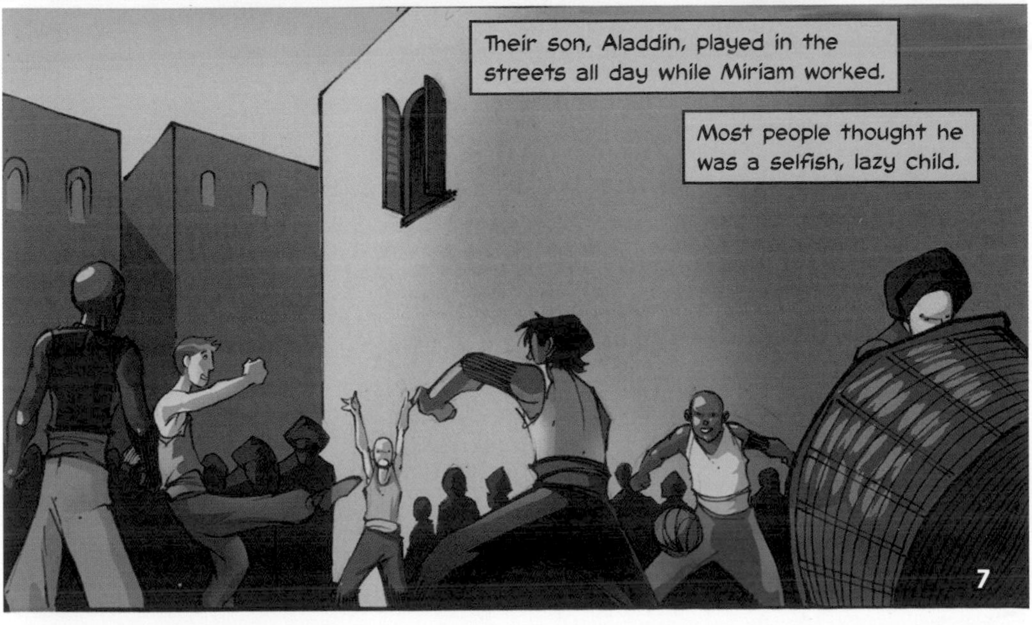
Their son, Aladdin, played in the streets all day while Miriam worked.
Most people thought he was a selfish, lazy child.

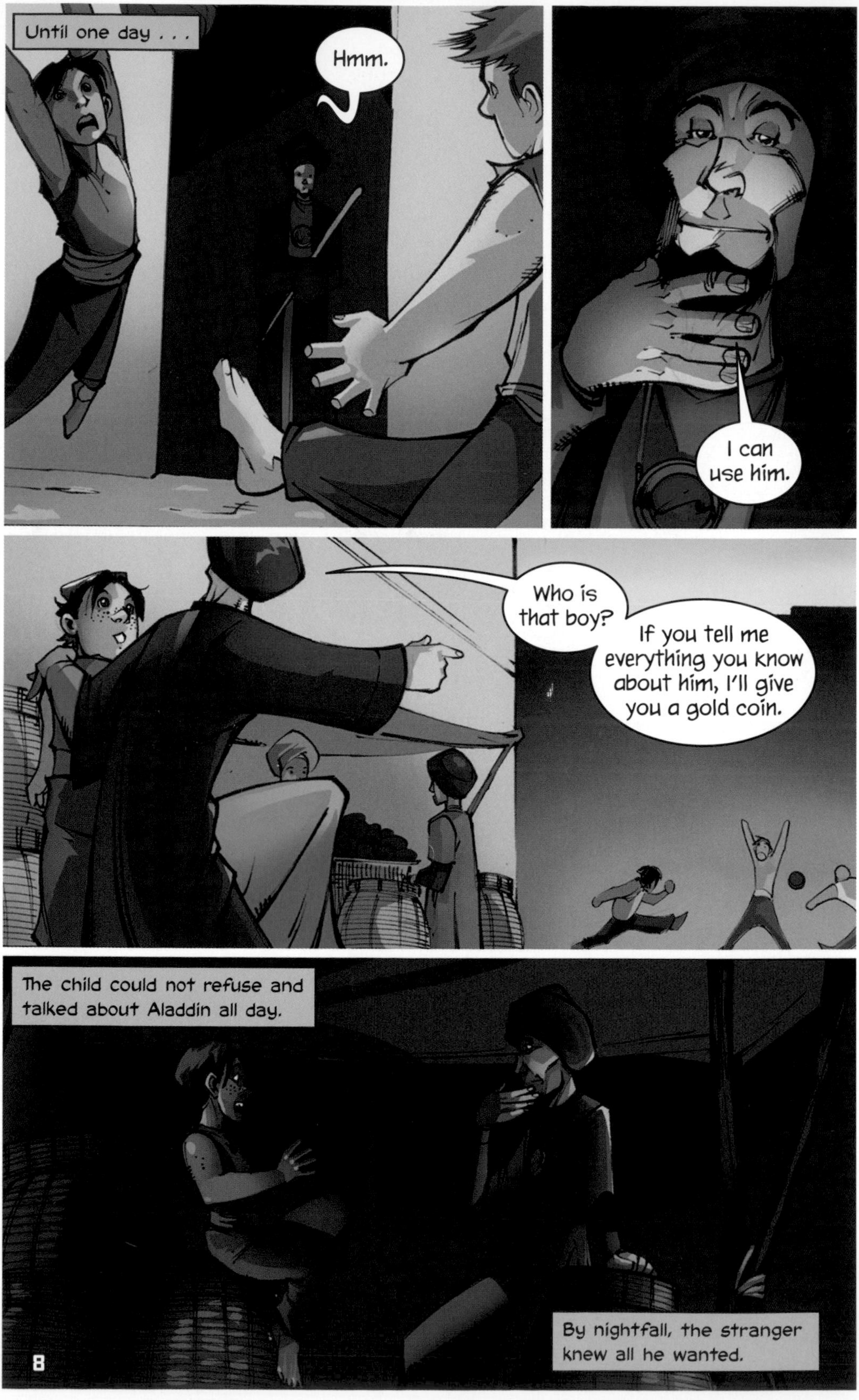

Until one day . . .
Hmm.
I can use him.
Who is that boy?
If you tell me everything you know about him, I'll give you a gold coin.
The child could not refuse and talked about Aladdin all day.
By nightfall, the stranger knew all he wanted.

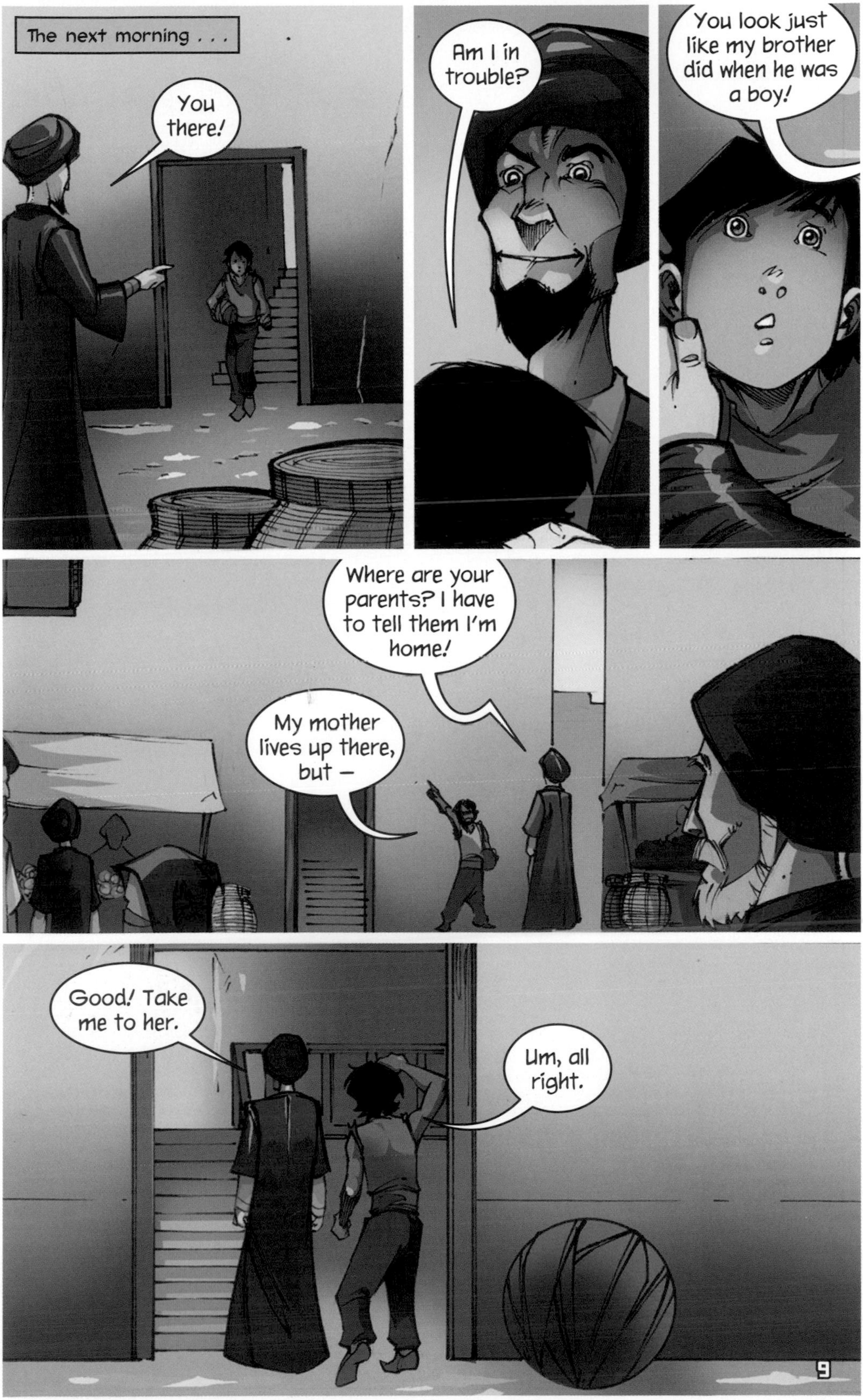
The next morning . . .
You there!
Am I in trouble?
You look just like my brother did when he was a boy!
Where are your parents? I have to tell them I'm home!
My mother lives up there, but –
Good! Take me to her.
Um, all right.

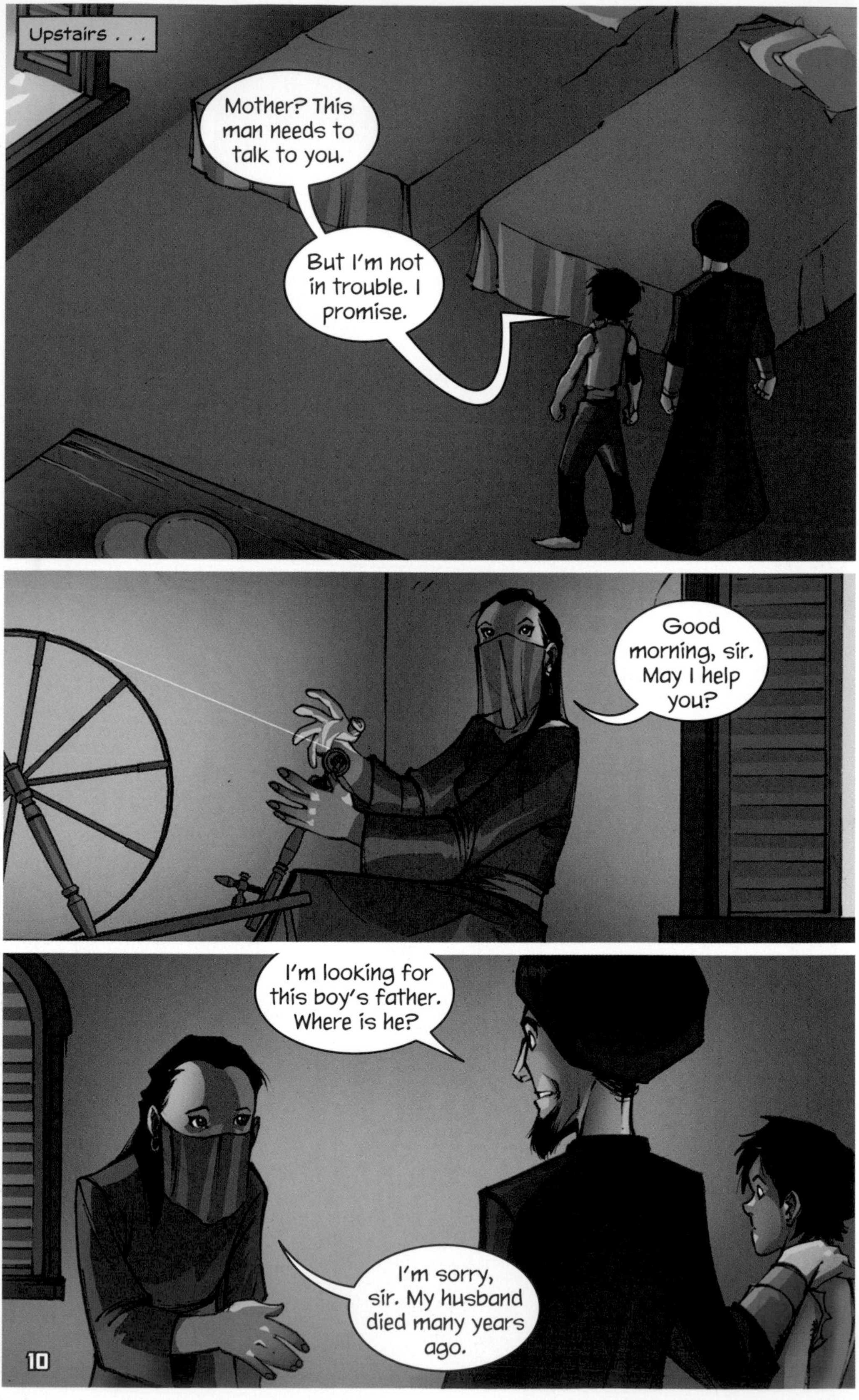
Upstairs . . .
Mother? This man needs to talk to you.
But I'm not in trouble. I promise.
Good morning, sir. May I help you?
I'm looking for this boy's father. Where is he?
I'm sorry, sir. My husband died many years ago.

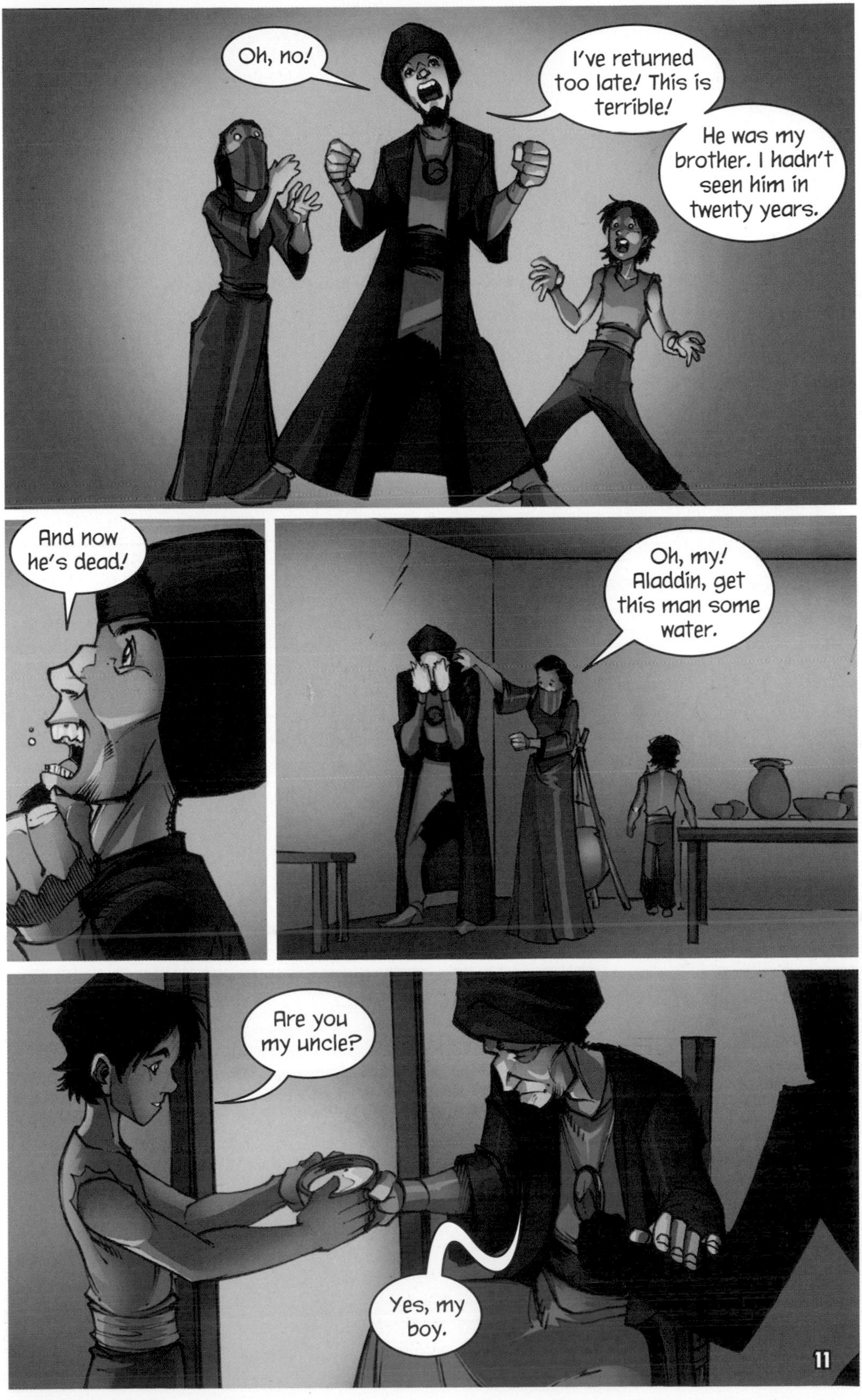
Oh, no!
I've returned too late! This is terrible!
He was my brother. I hadn't seen him in twenty years.
And now he's dead!
Oh, my! Aladdin, get this man some water.
Are you my uncle?
Yes, my boy.

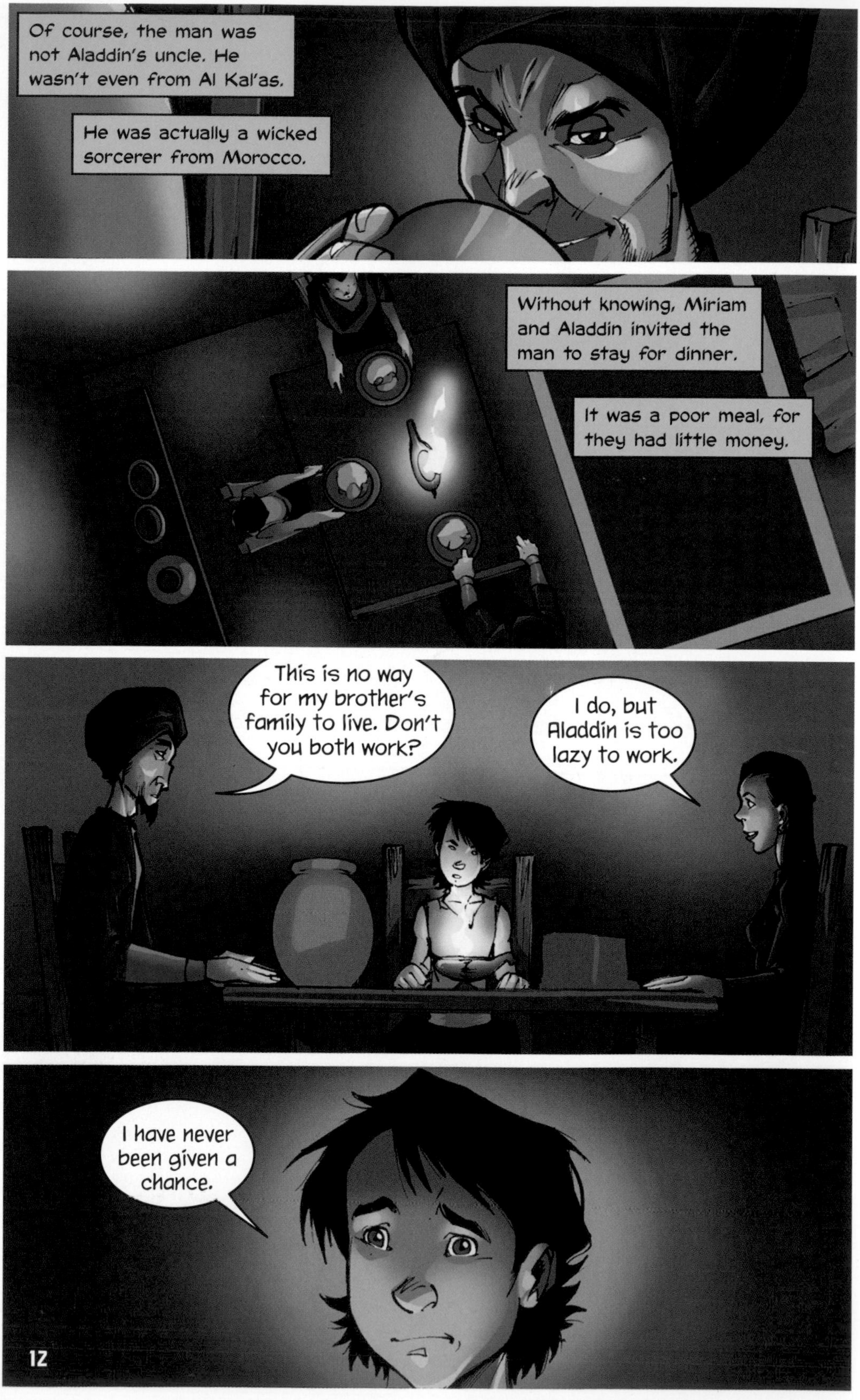
Of course, the man was not Aladdin's uncle. He wasn't even from Al Kal'as.
He was actually a wicked sorcerer from Morocco.
Without knowing, Miriam and Aladdin invited the man to stay for dinner.
It was a poor meal, for they had little money.
This is no way for my brother's family to live. Don't you both work?
I do, but Aladdin is too lazy to work.
I have never been given a chance.

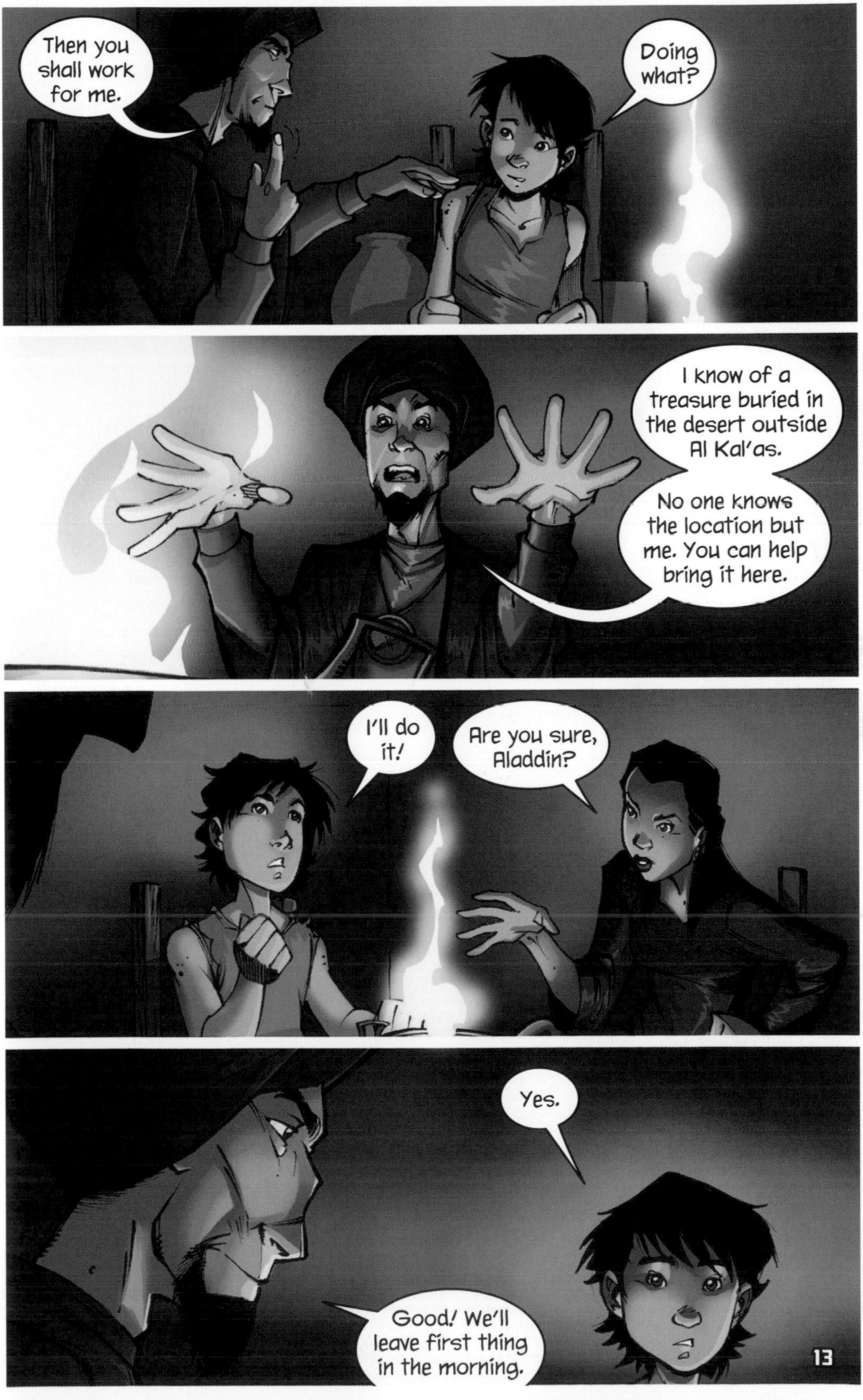
Then you shall work for me.
Doing what?
I know of a treasure buried in the desert outside Al Kal'as.
No one knows the location but me. You can help bring it here.
I'll do it!
Are you sure, Aladdin?
Yes.
Good! We'll leave first thing in the morning.

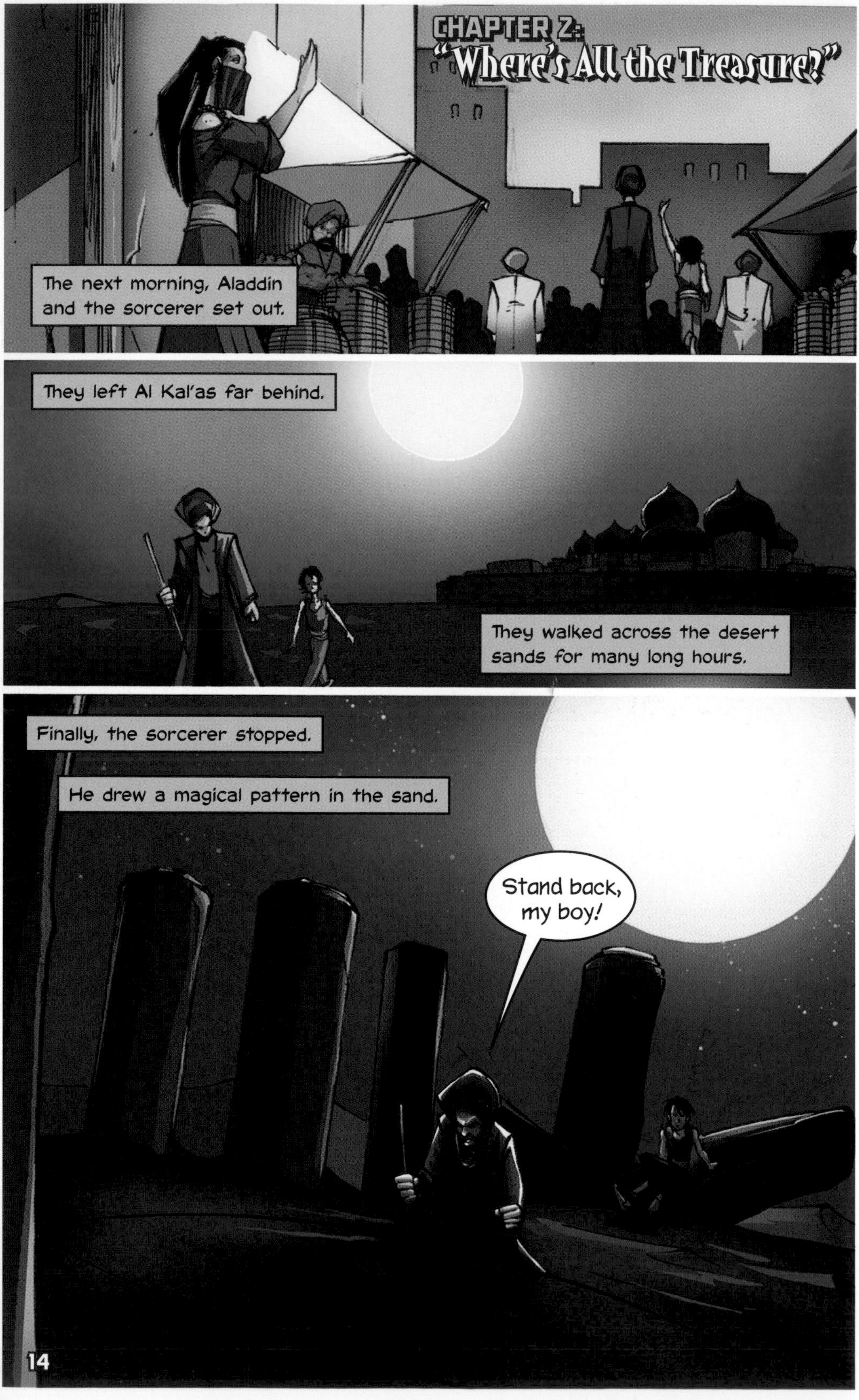
CHAPTER 2:
"Where's All the Treasure?"
The next morning, Aladdin and the sorcerer set out.
They left Al Kal'as far behind.
They walked across the desert sands for many long hours.
Finally, the sorcerer stopped.
He drew a magical pattern in the sand.
Stand back, my boy!

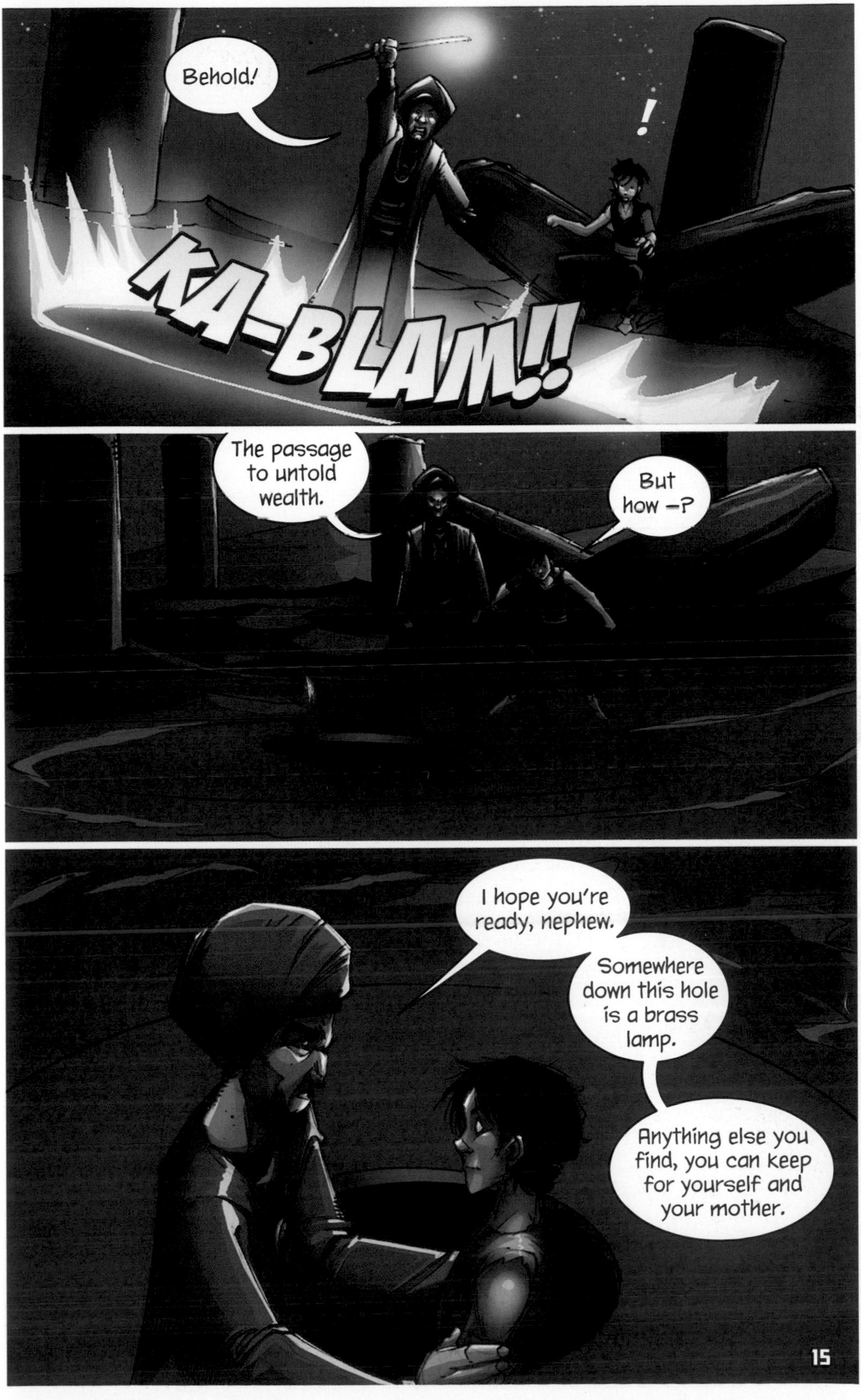
Behold!
!
KA-BLAM!!
The passage to untold wealth.
But how —?
I hope you're ready, nephew.
Somewhere down this hole is a brass lamp.
Anything else you find, you can keep for yourself and your mother.

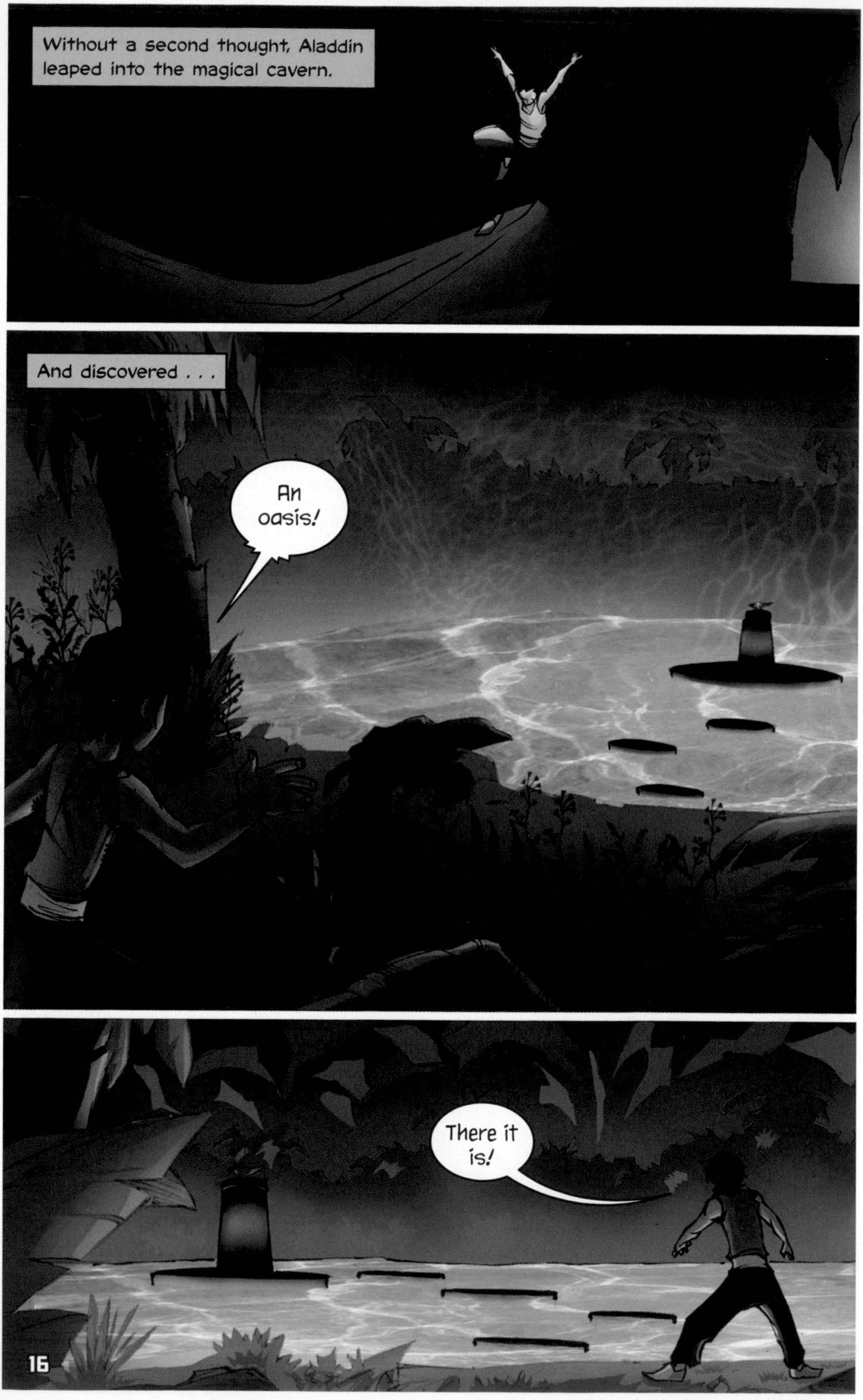
Without a second thought, Aladdin leaped into the magical cavern.
And discovered . . .
An oasis!
There it is!

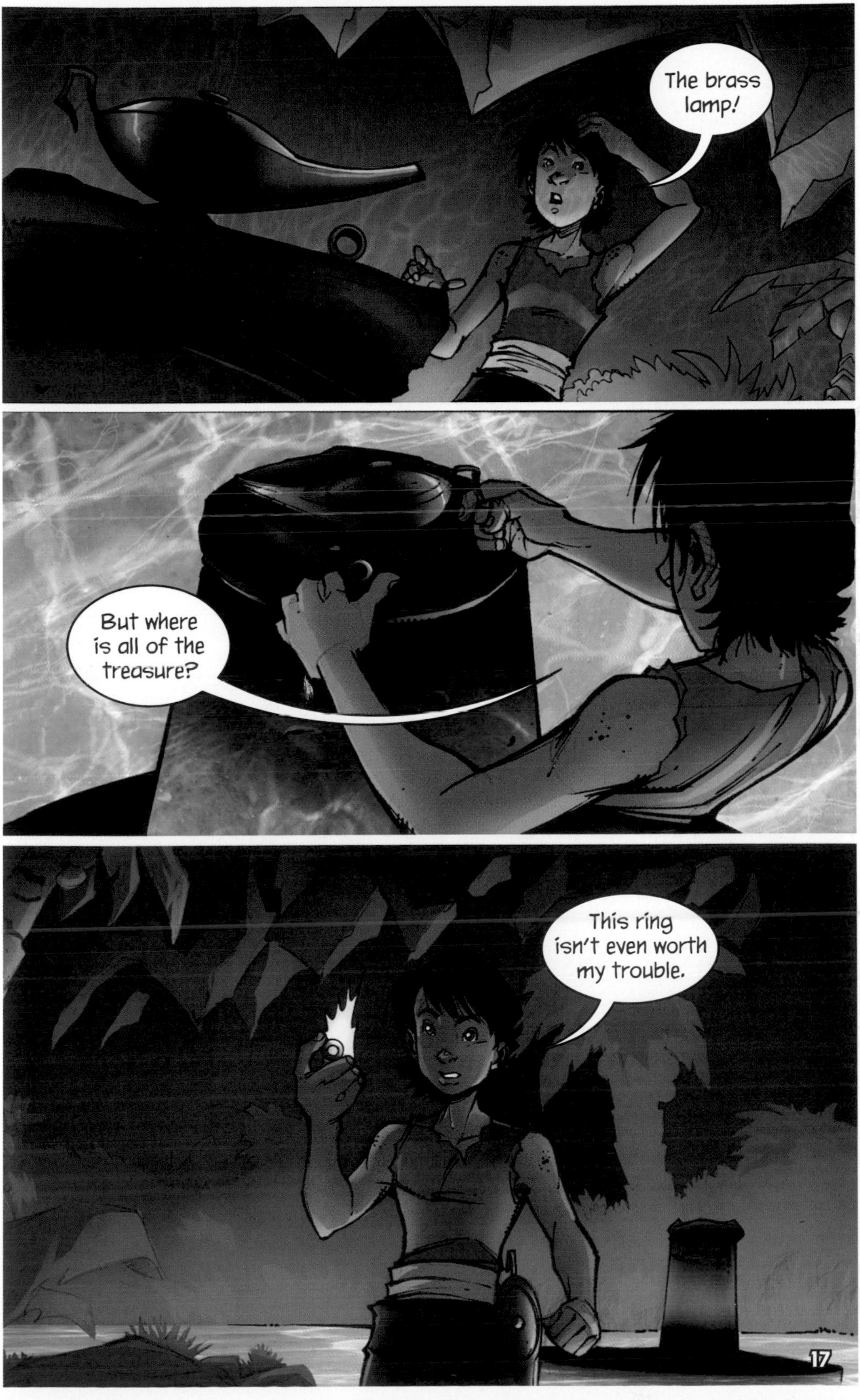

The brass lamp!
But where is all of the treasure?
This ring isn't even worth my trouble.

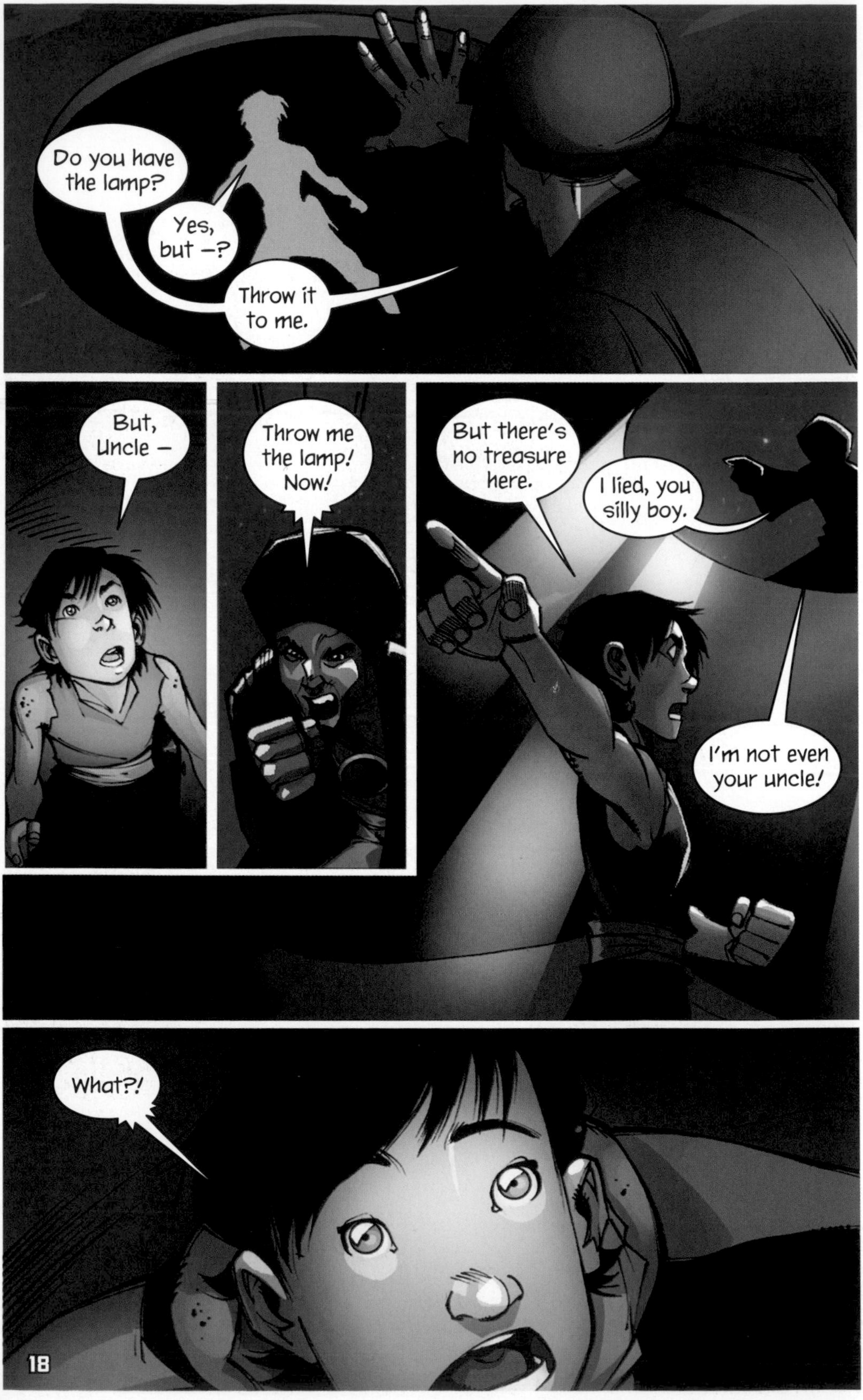
Do you have the lamp?
Yes, but —?
Throw it to me.
But, Uncle —
Throw me the lamp! Now!
But there's no treasure here.
I lied, you silly boy.
I'm not even your uncle!
What?!

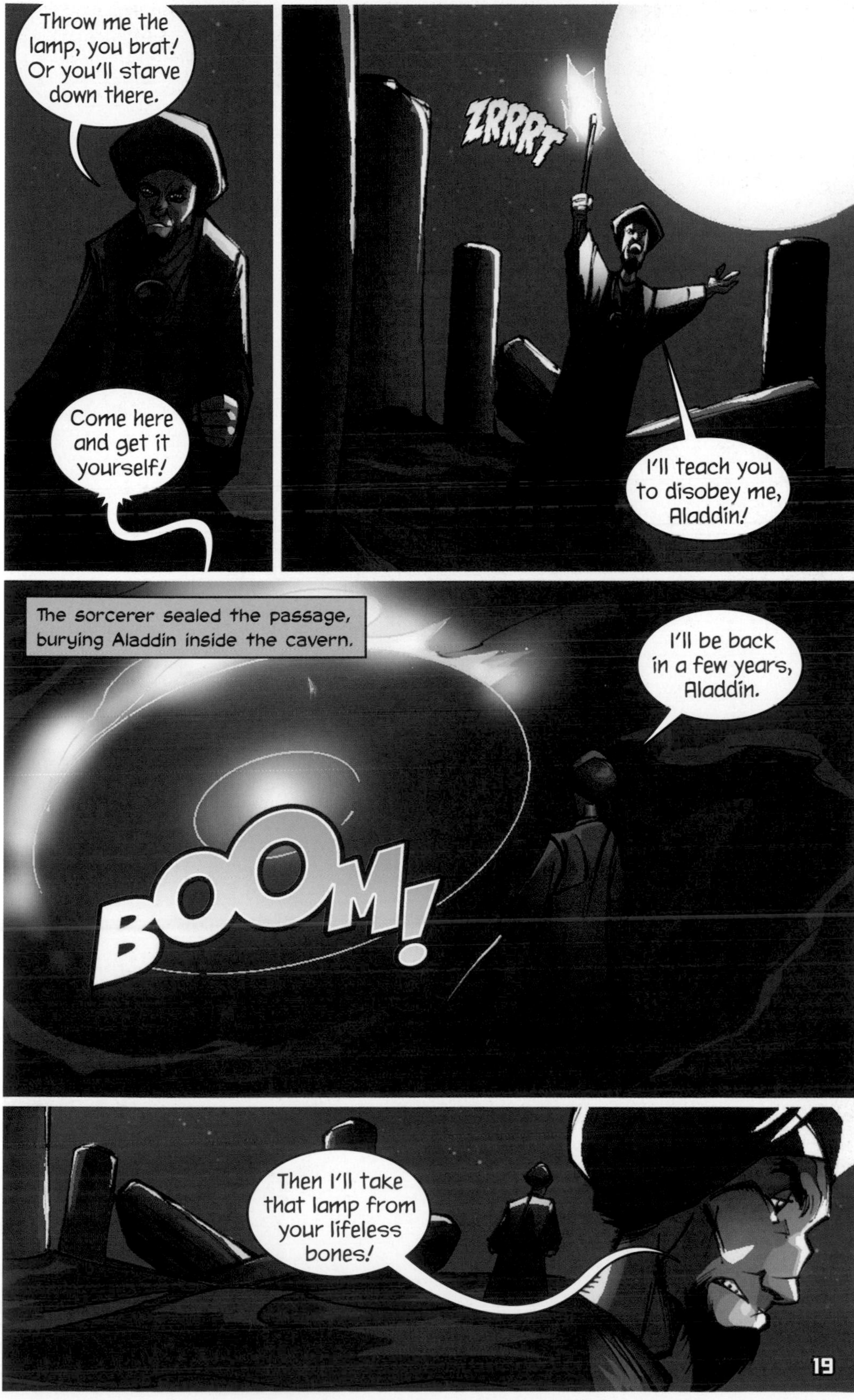
Throw me the lamp, you brat! Or you'll starve down there.
Come here and get it yourself!
ZRRRT
I'll teach you to disobey me, Aladdin!
The sorcerer sealed the passage, burying Aladdin inside the cavern.
I'll be back in a few years, Aladdin.
BOOM!
Then I'll take that lamp from your lifeless bones!

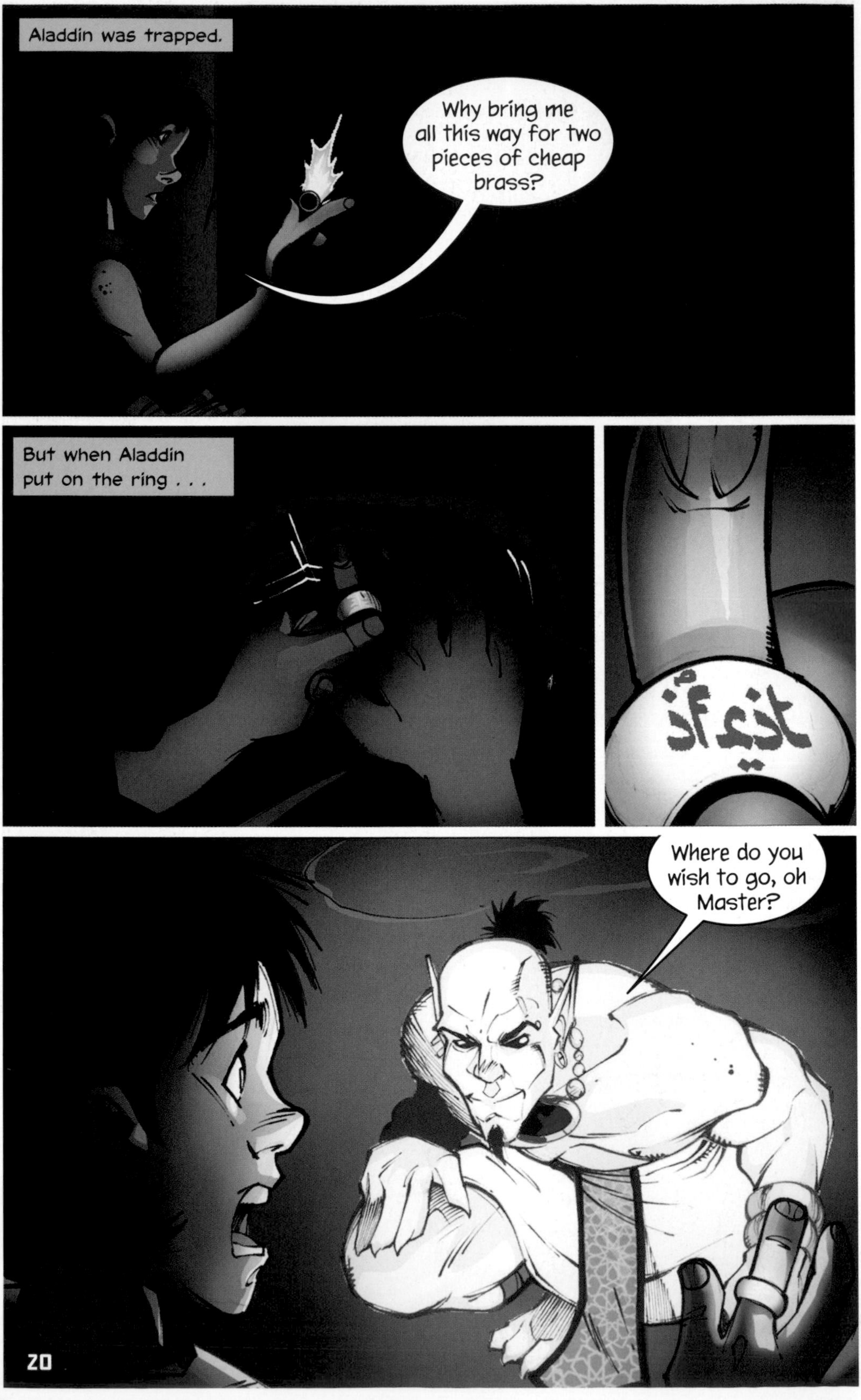
Aladdin was trapped.
Why bring me all this way for two pieces of cheap brass?
But when Aladdin put on the ring . . .
Where do you wish to go, oh Master?

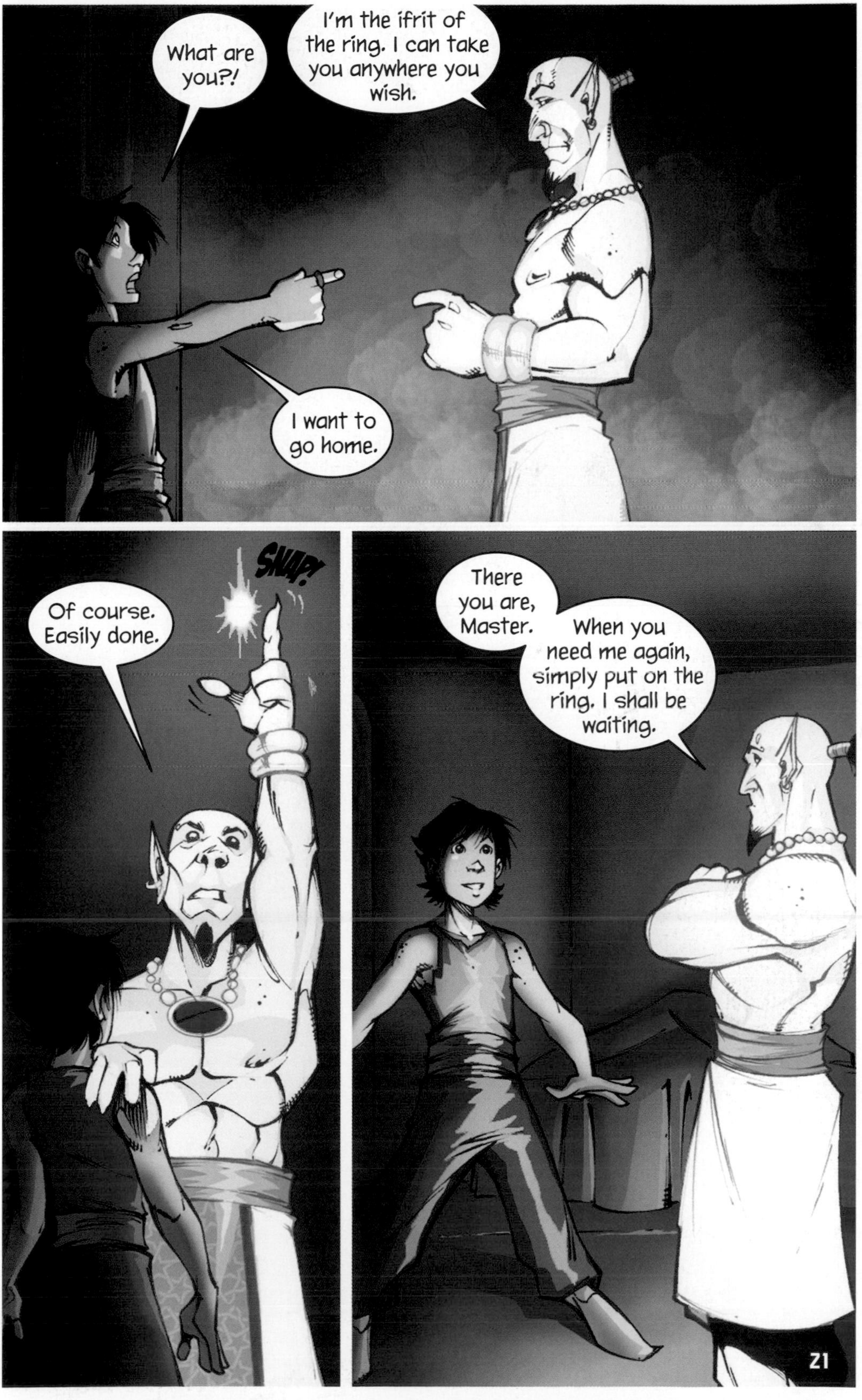
What are you?!
I'm the ifrit of the ring. I can take you anywhere you wish.
I want to go home.
Of course. Easily done.
SNAP!
There you are, Master.
When you need me again, simply put on the ring. I shall be waiting.

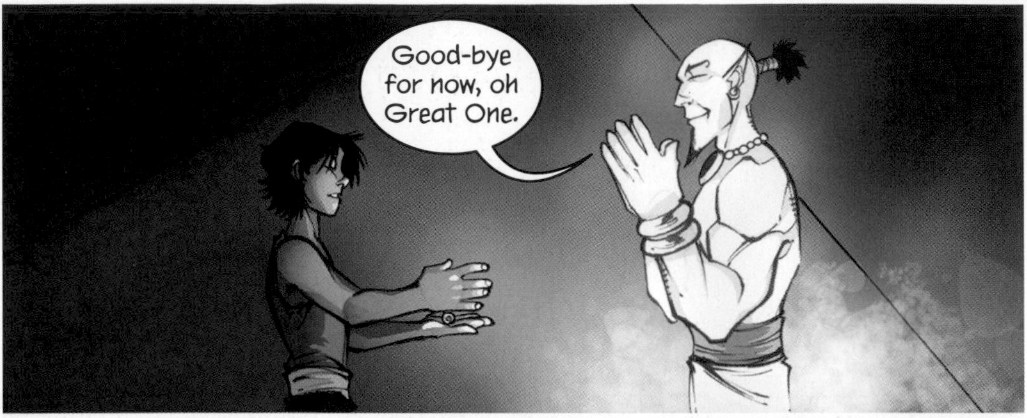
Good-bye for now, oh Great One.

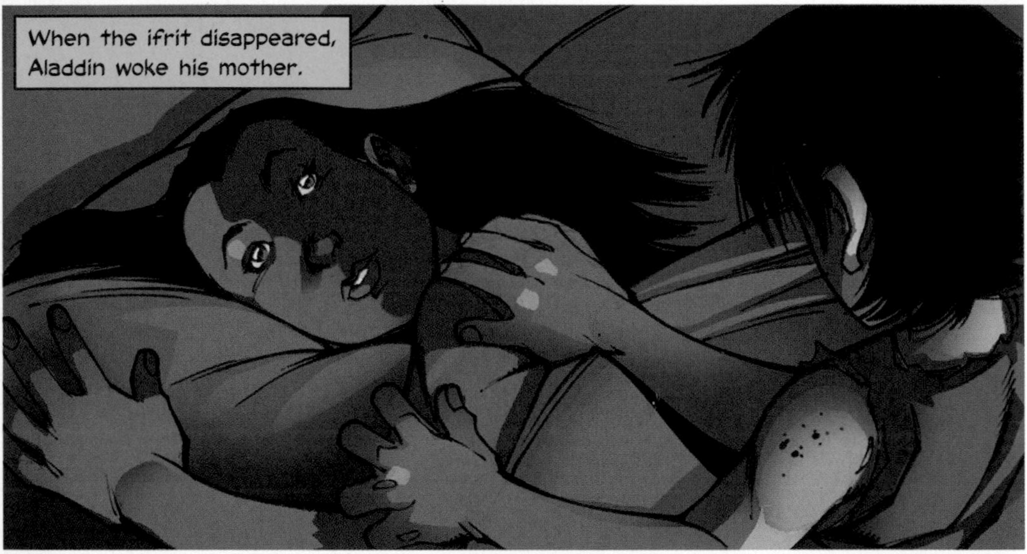
When the ifrit disappeared, Aladdin woke his mother.

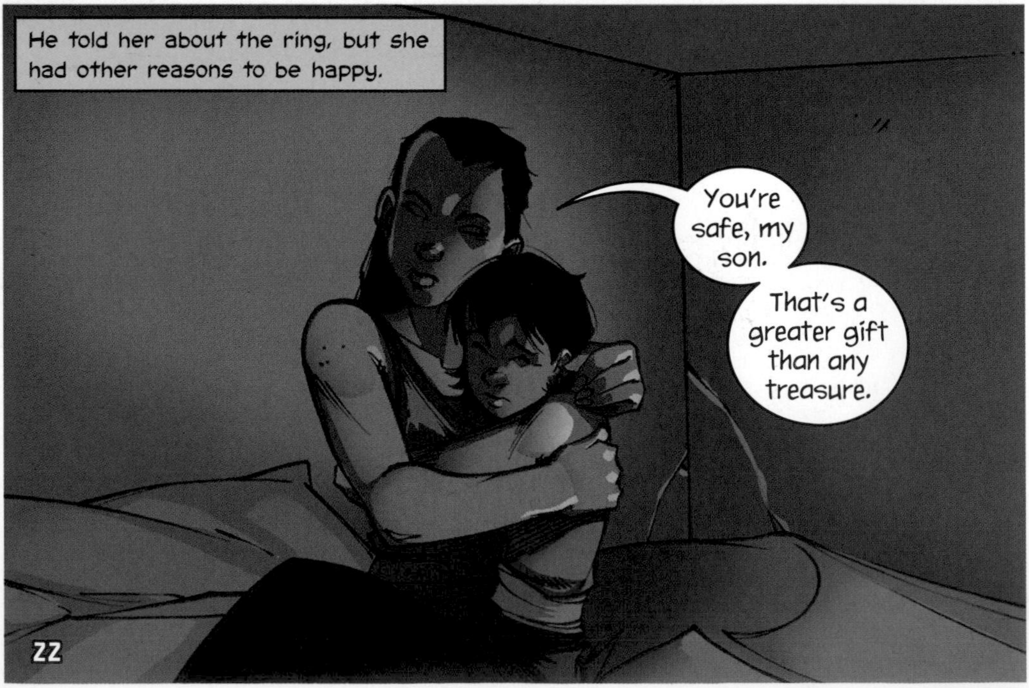
He told her about the ring, but she had other reasons to be happy.
You're safe, my son.
That's a greater gift than any treasure.

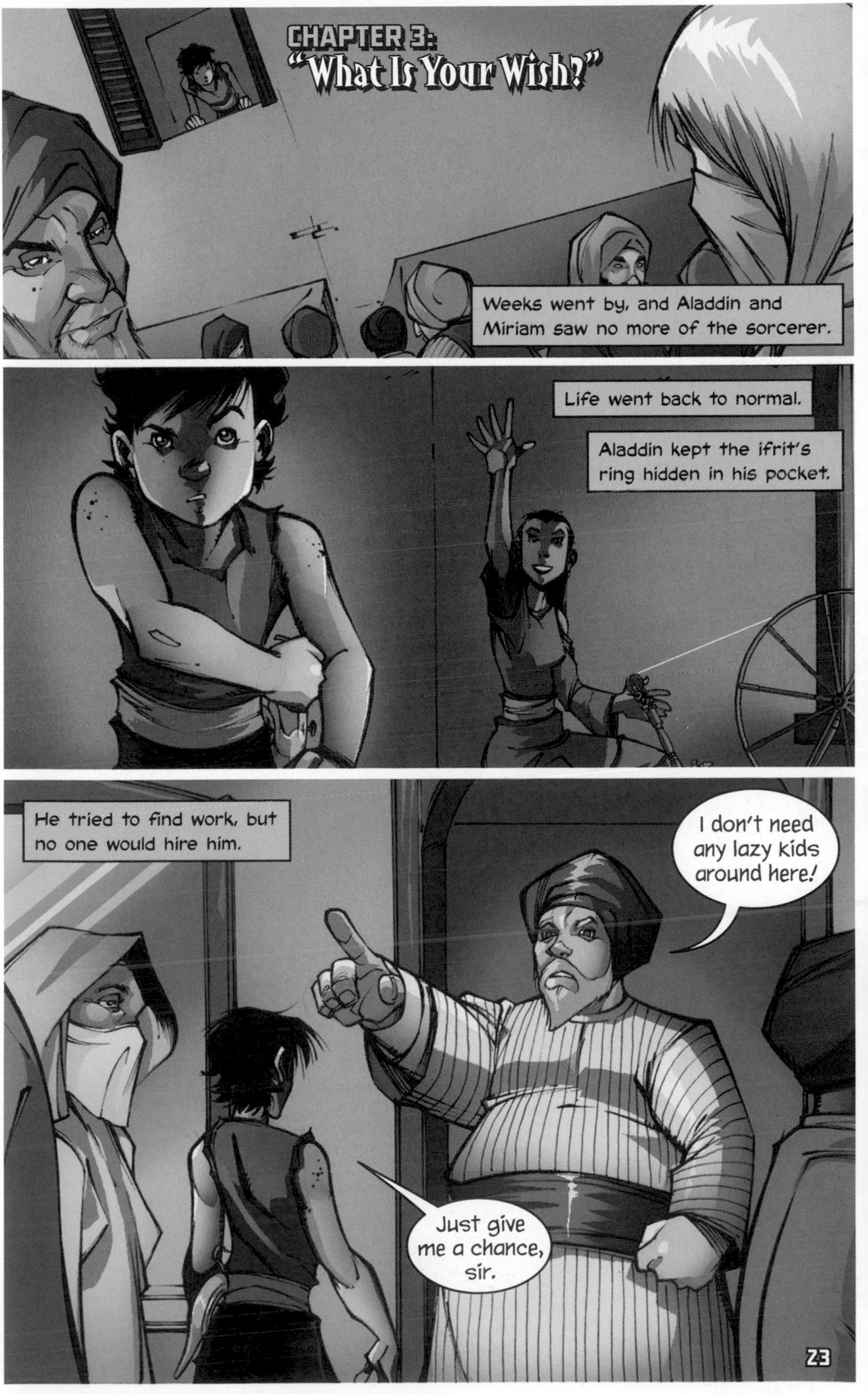
CHAPTER 3:
"What Is Your Wish?"
Weeks went by, and Aladdin and Miriam saw no more of the sorcerer.
Life went back to normal.
Aladdin kept the ifrit's ring hidden in his pocket.
He tried to find work, but no one would hire him.
I don't need any lazy kids around here!
Just give me a chance, sir.

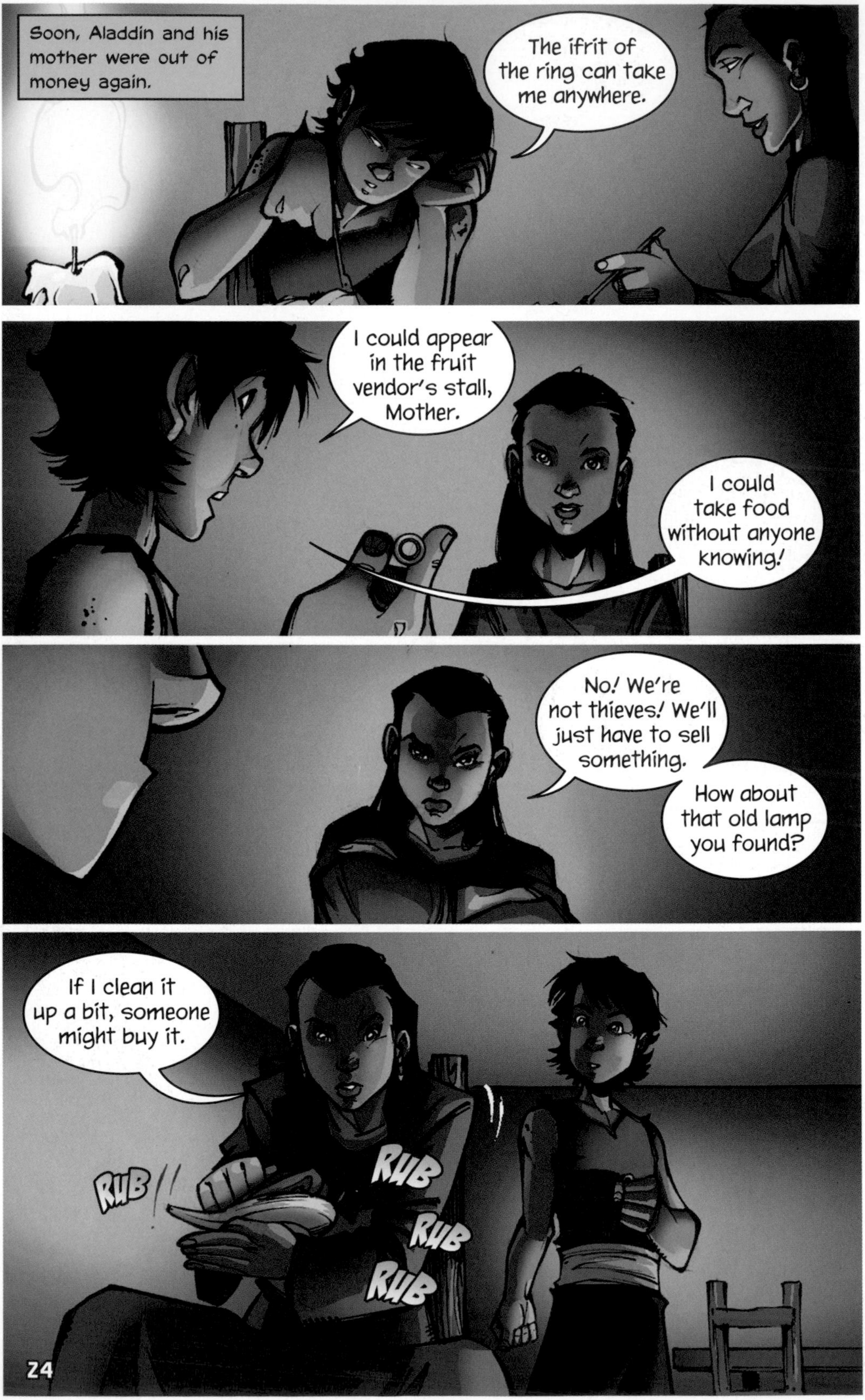

Soon, Aladdin and his mother were out of money again.
The ifrit of the ring can take me anywhere.
I could appear in the fruit vendor's stall, Mother.
I could take food without anyone knowing!
No! We're not thieves! We'll just have to sell something.
How about that old lamp you found?
If I clean it up a bit, someone might buy it.
RUB
RUB
RUB
RUB

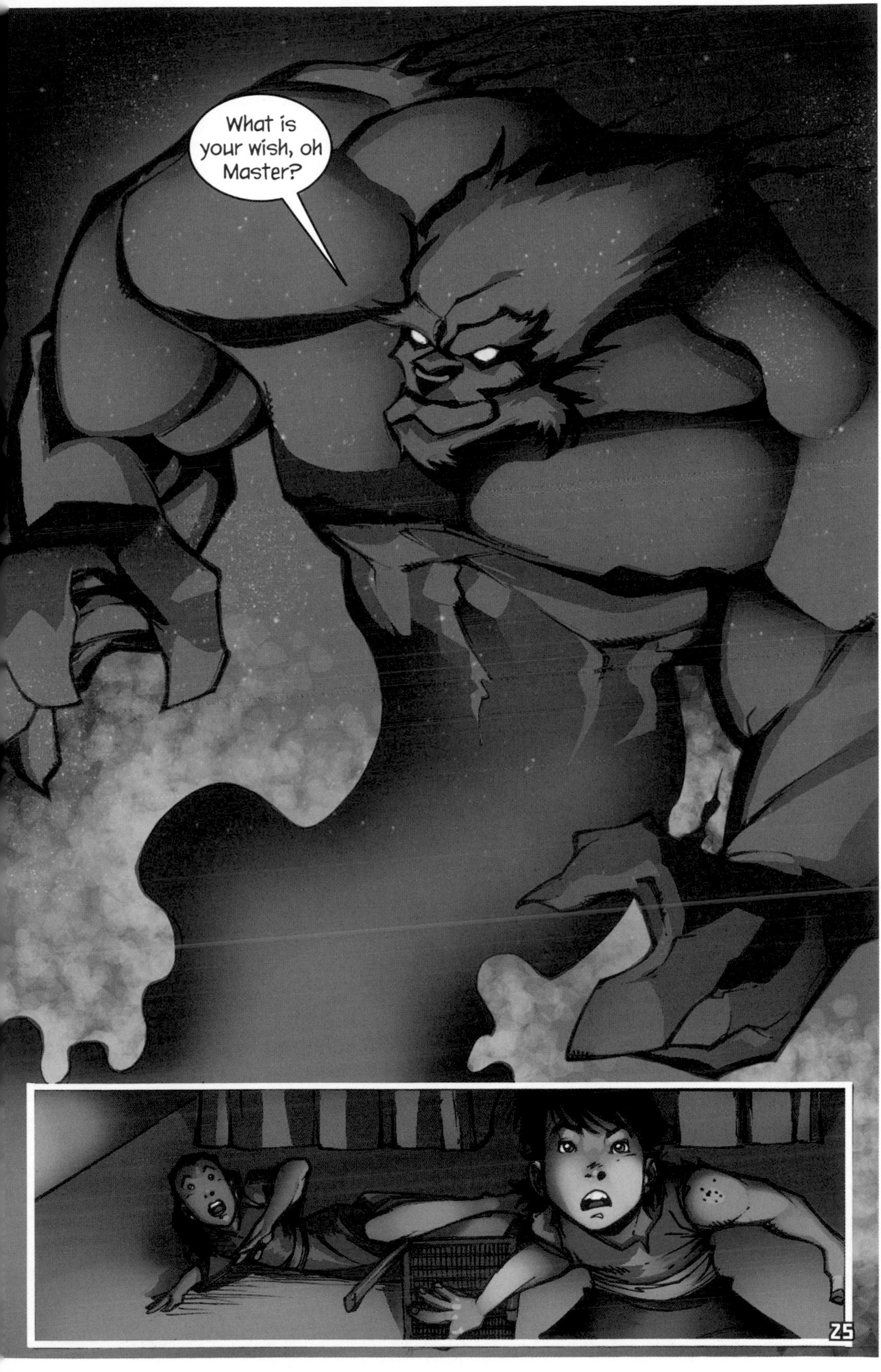
What is your wish, oh Master?

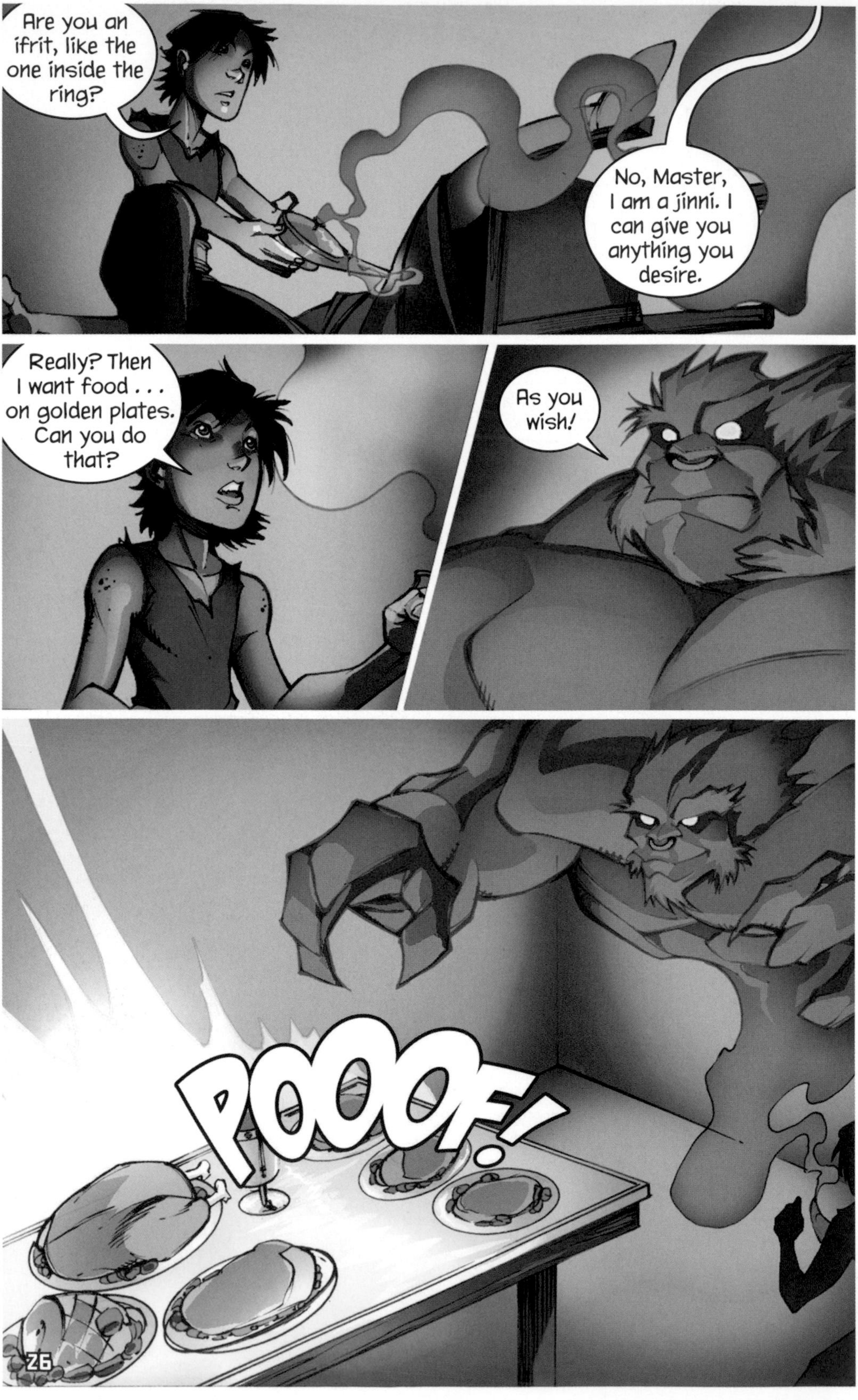

Are you an ifrit, like the one inside the ring?
No, Master, I am a jinni. I can give you anything you desire.
Really? Then I want food . . . on golden plates. Can you do that?
As you wish!
POOOF!

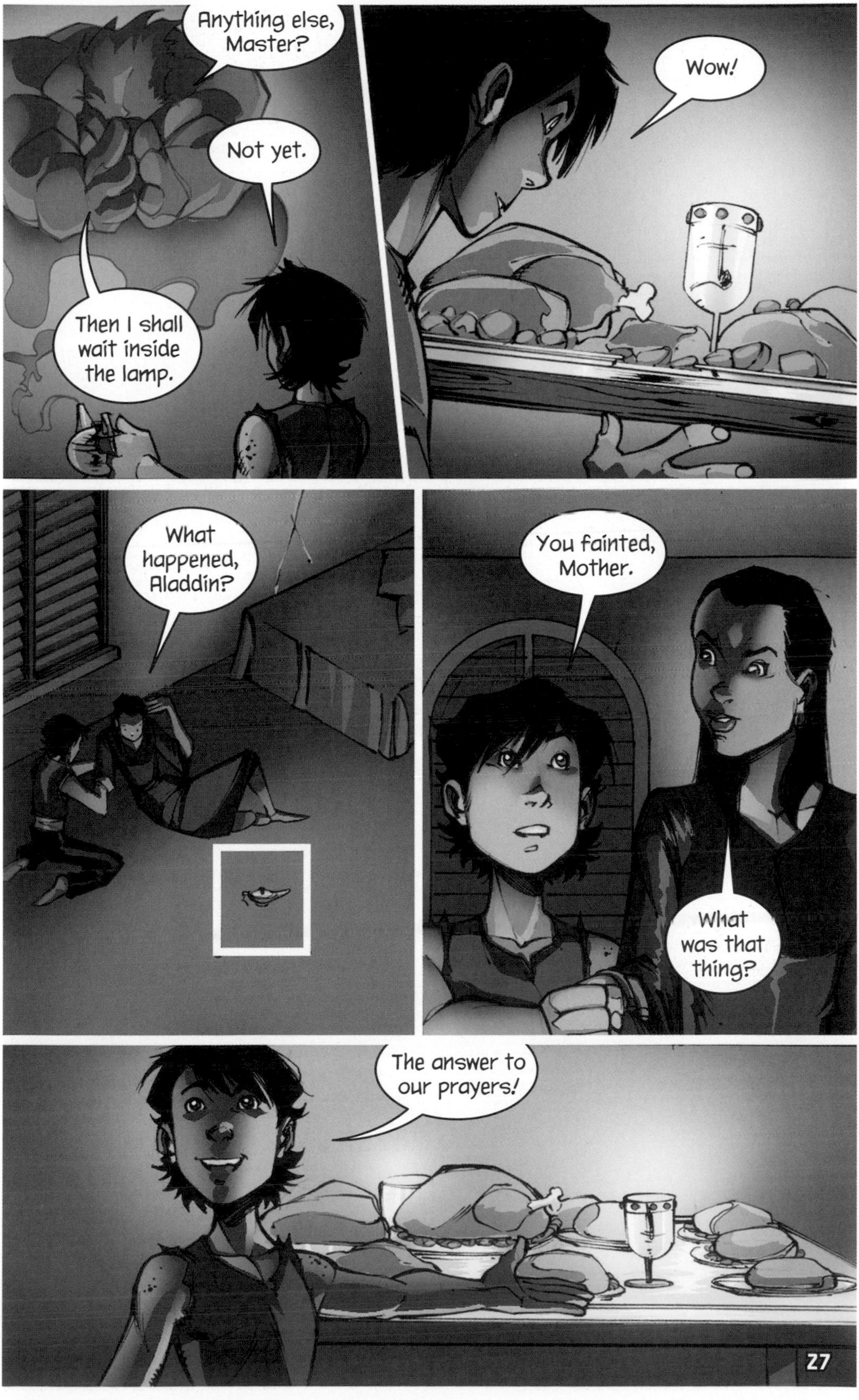
Anything else, Master?
Not yet.
Then I shall wait inside the lamp.
Wow!
What happened, Aladdin?
You fainted, Mother.
What was that thing?
The answer to our prayers!

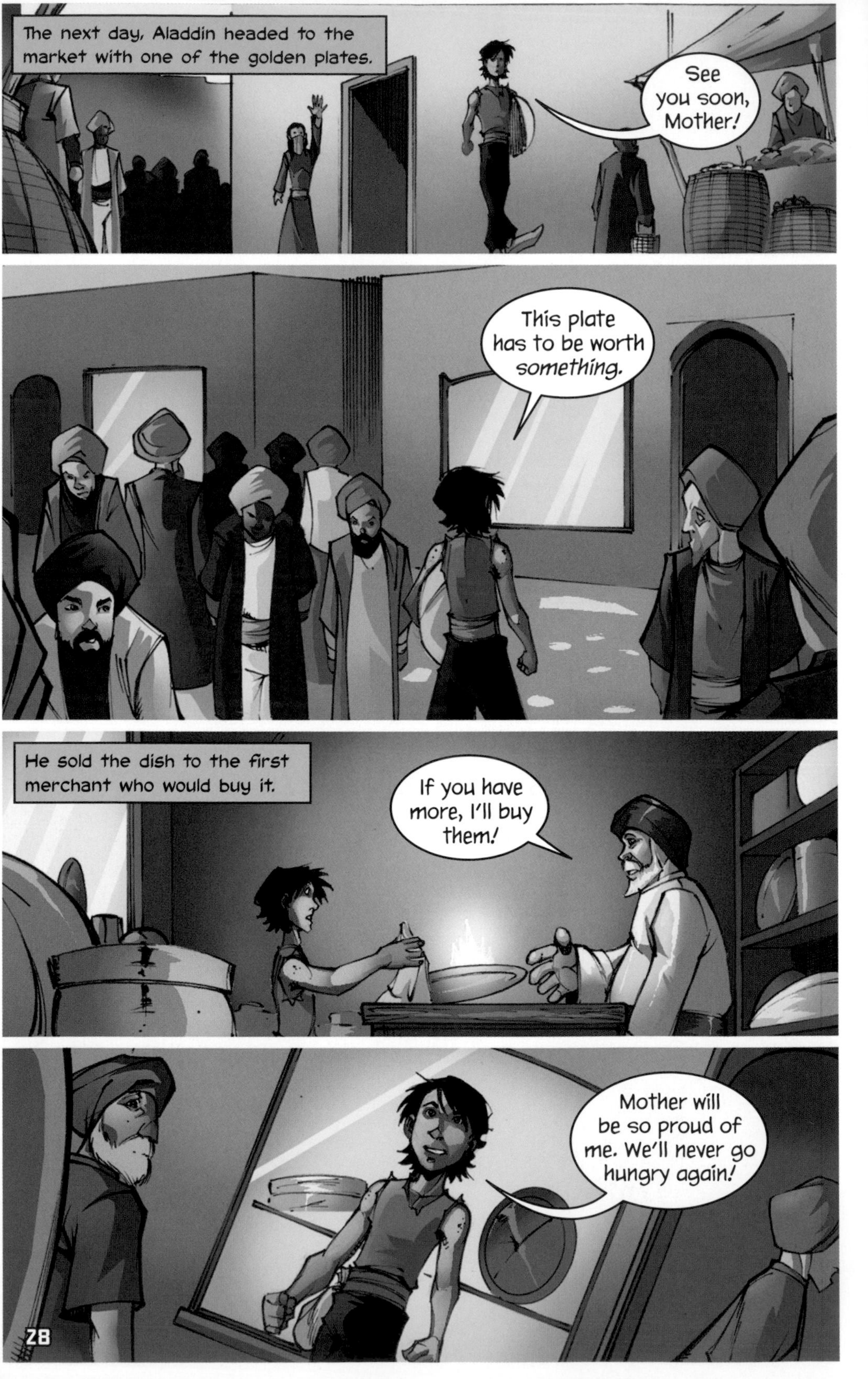
The next day, Aladdin headed to the market with one of the golden plates.
See you soon, Mother!
This plate has to be worth *something.*
He sold the dish to the first merchant who would buy it.
If you have more, I'll buy them!
Mother will be so proud of me. We'll never go hungry again!

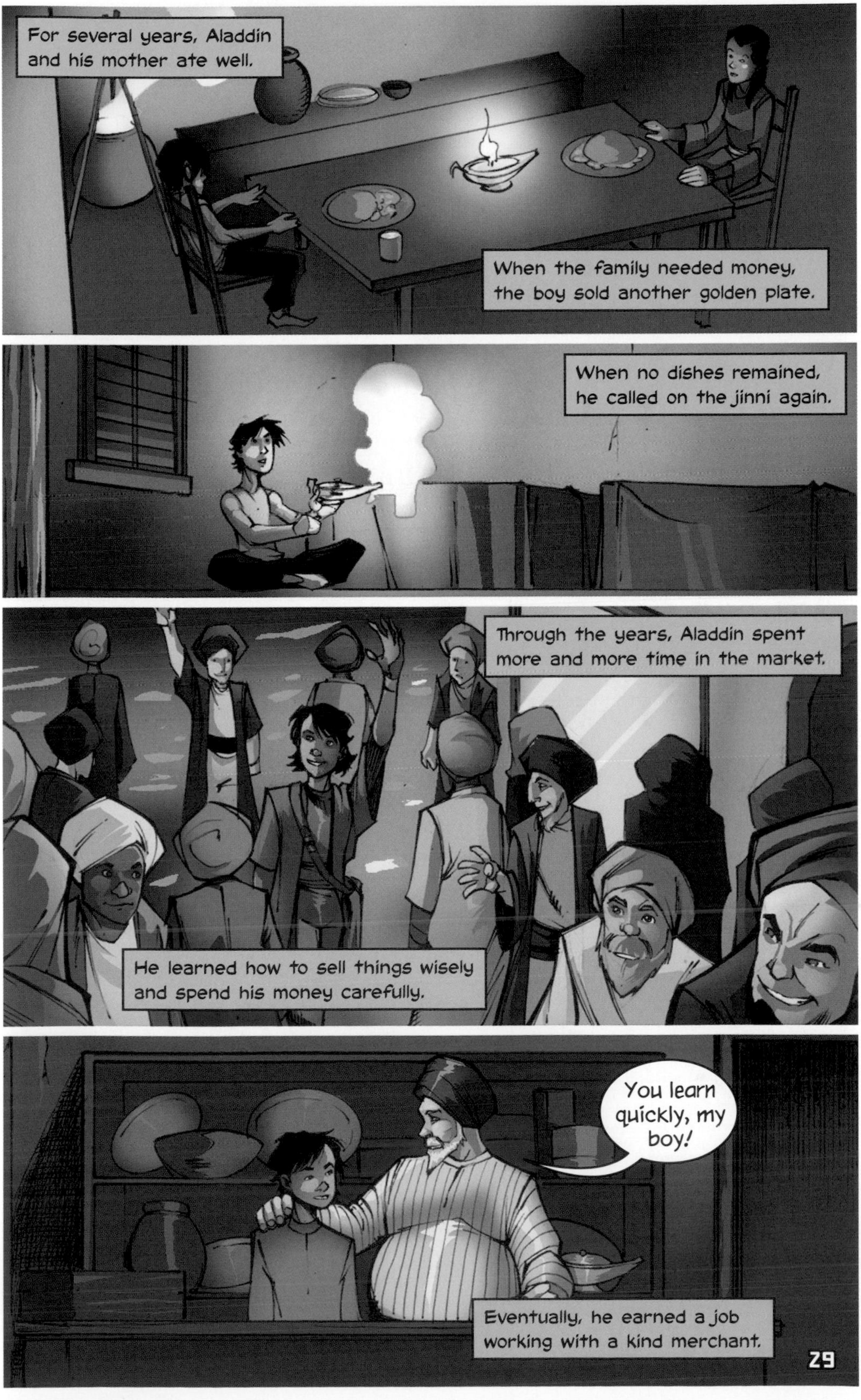
For several years, Aladdin and his mother ate well.
When the family needed money, the boy sold another golden plate.
When no dishes remained, he called on the jinni again.
Through the years, Aladdin spent more and more time in the market.
He learned how to sell things wisely and spend his money carefully.
You learn quickly, my boy!
Eventually, he earned a job working with a kind merchant.

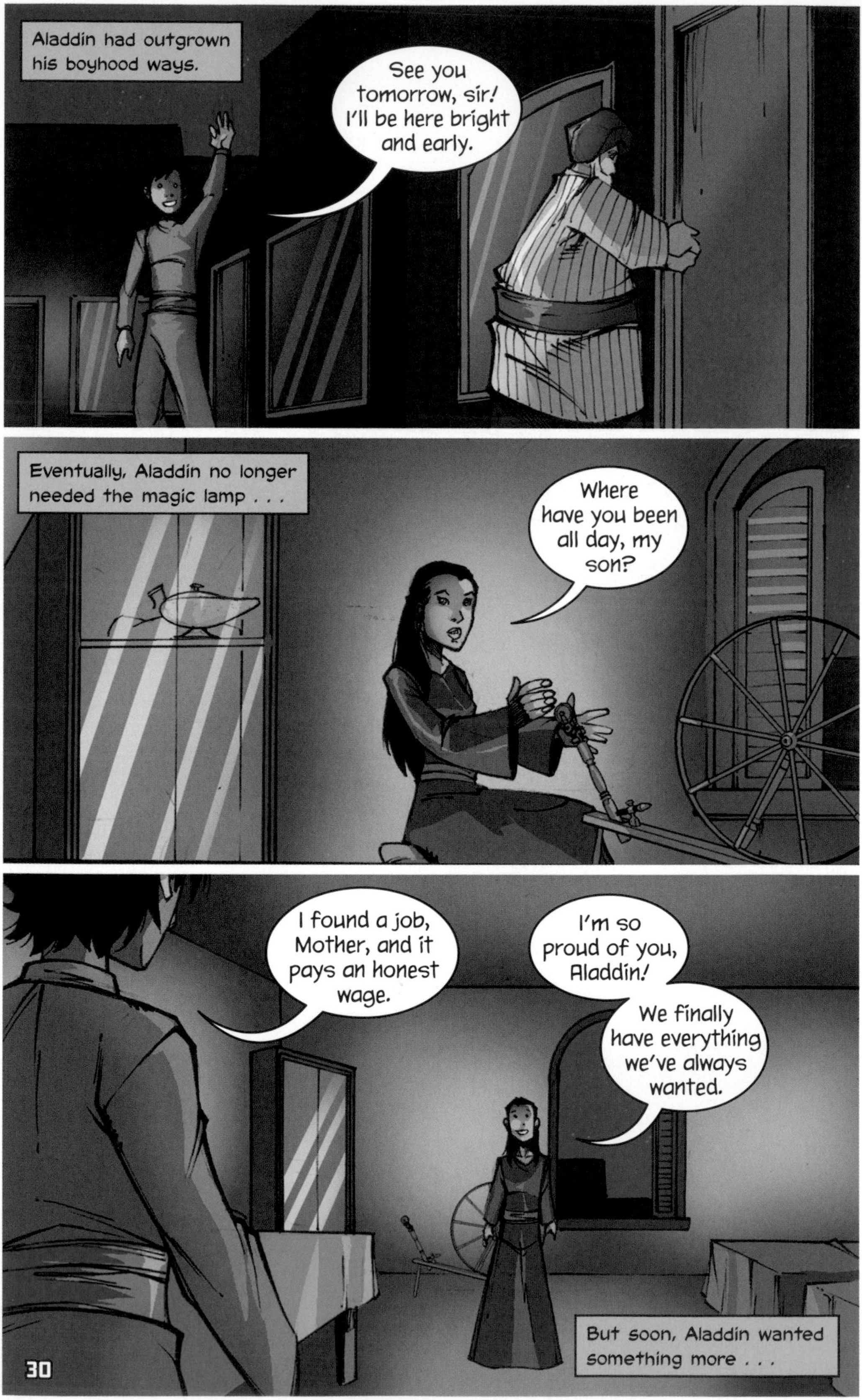
Aladdin had outgrown his boyhood ways.
See you tomorrow, sir! I'll be here bright and early.
Eventually, Aladdin no longer needed the magic lamp . . .
Where have you been all day, my son?
I found a job, Mother, and it pays an honest wage.
I'm so proud of you, Aladdin!
We finally have everything we've always wanted.
But soon, Aladdin wanted something more . . .

CHAPTER 4: "From Love"

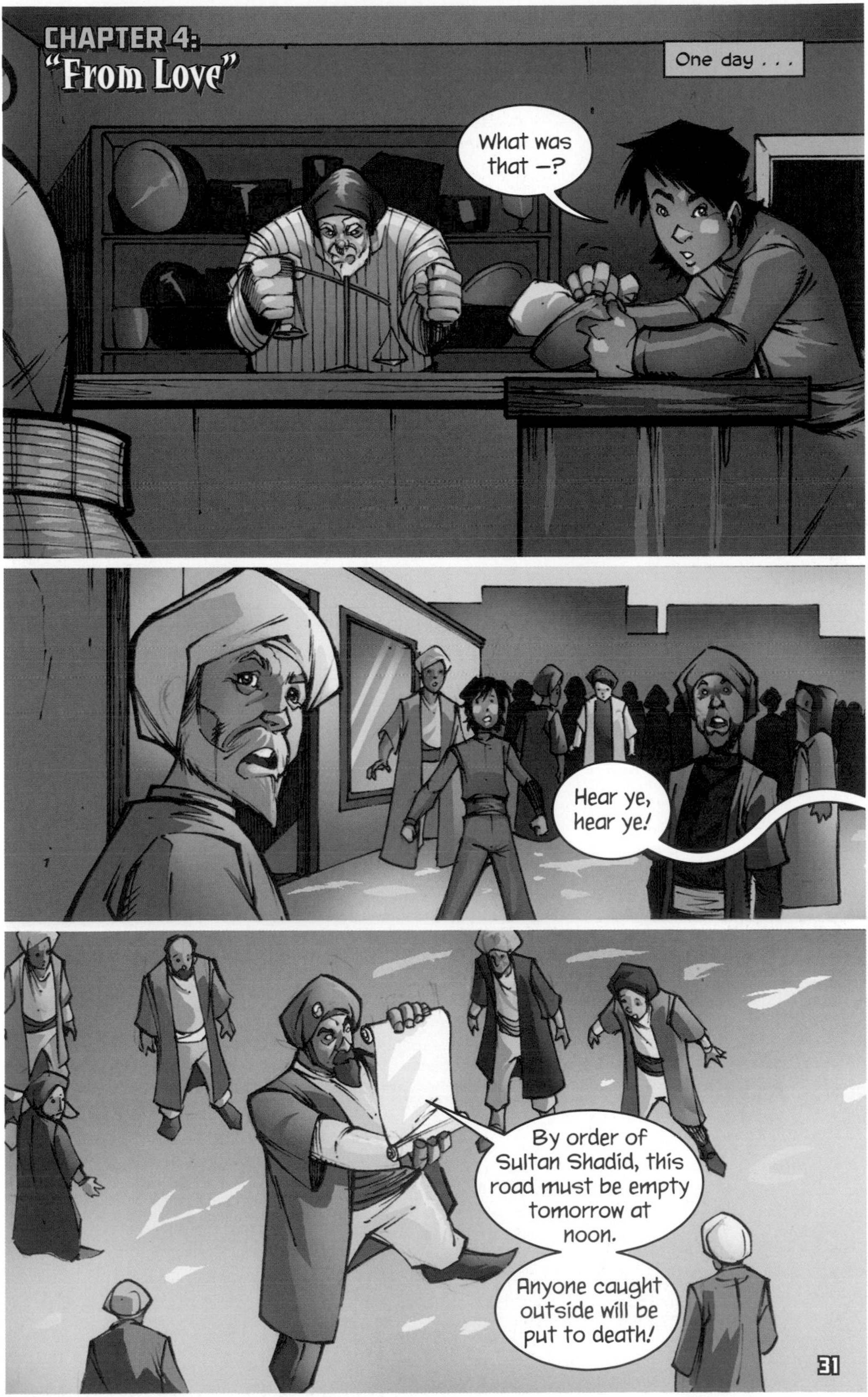
One day . . .
What was that —?
Hear ye, hear ye!
By order of Sultan Shadid, this road must be empty tomorrow at noon.
Anyone caught outside will be put to death!

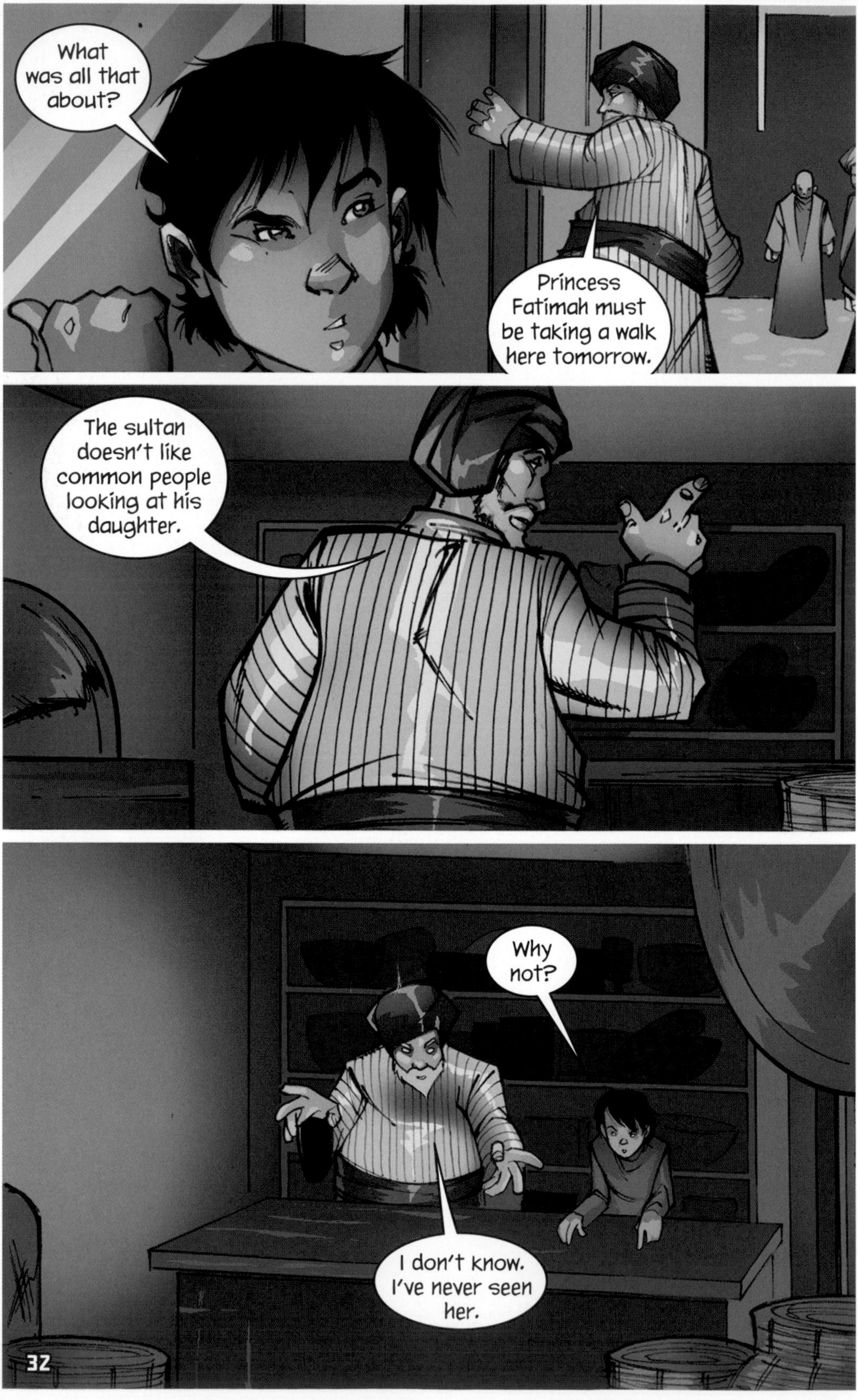
What was all that about?
Princess Fatimah must be taking a walk here tomorrow.
The sultan doesn't like common people looking at his daughter.
Why not?
I don't know. I've never seen her.

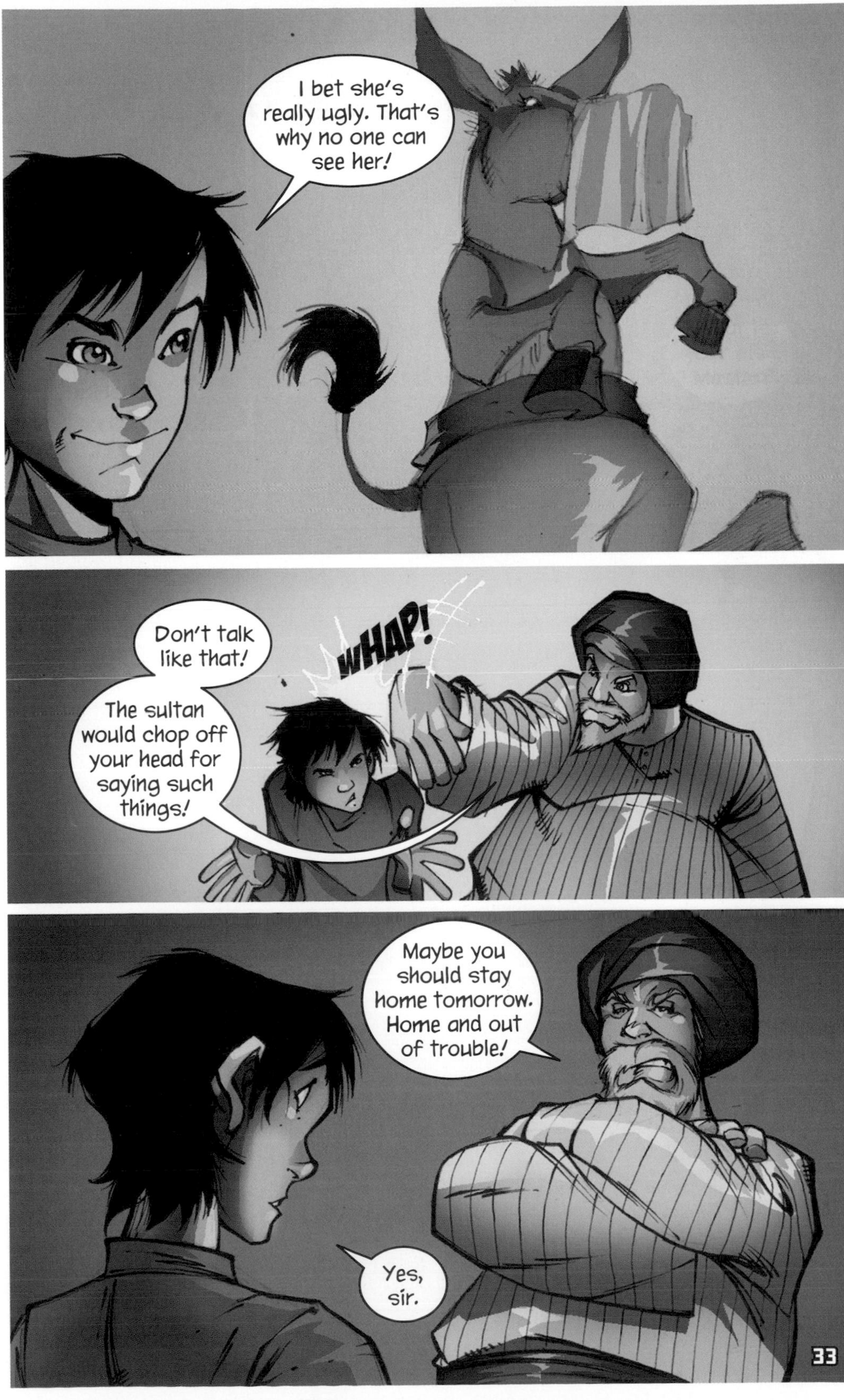
I bet she's really ugly. That's why no one can see her!
Don't talk like that!
WHAP!
The sultan would chop off your head for saying such things!
Maybe you should stay home tomorrow. Home and out of trouble!
Yes, sir.

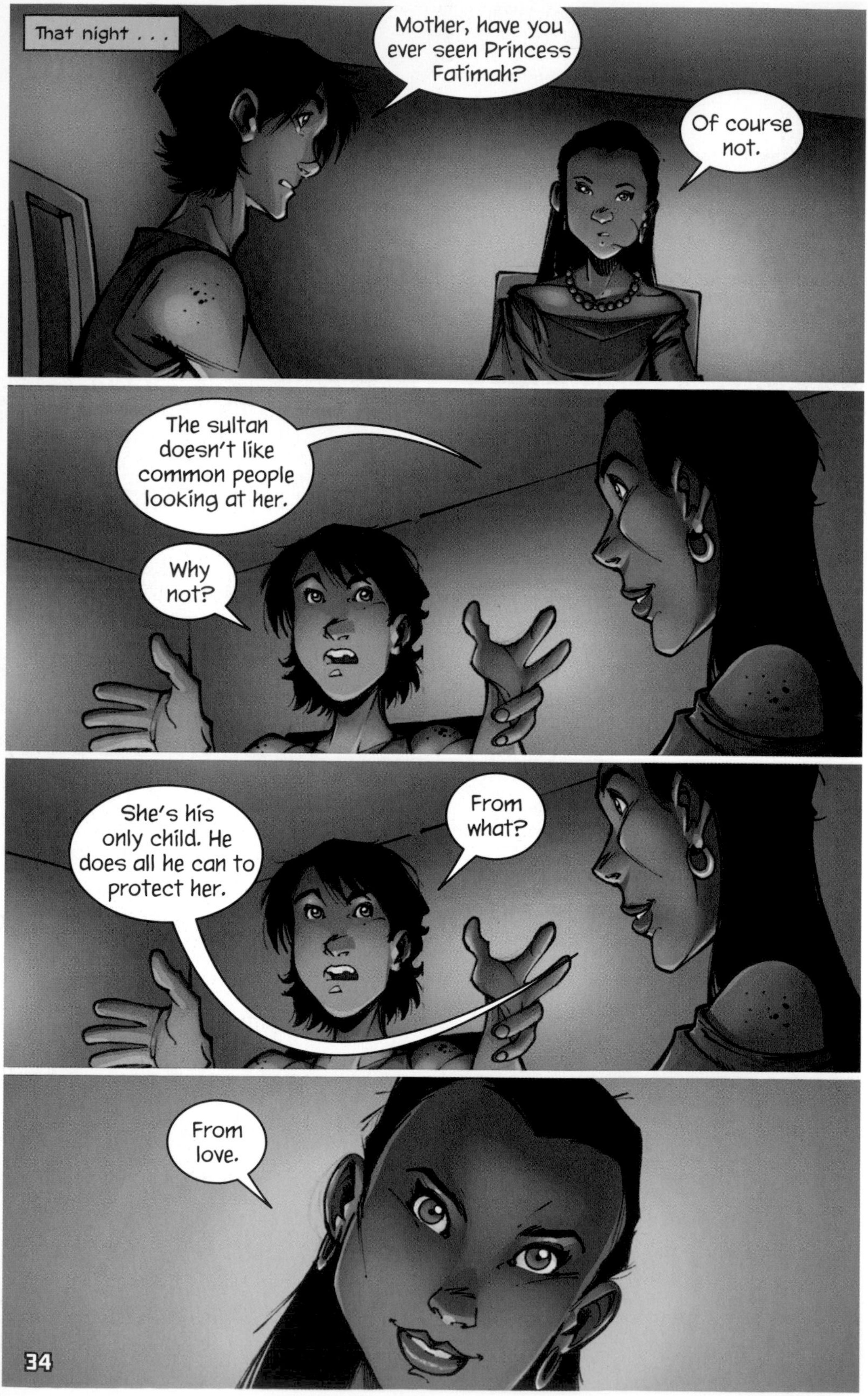

That night . . .
Mother, have you ever seen Princess Fatimah?
Of course not.
The sultan doesn't like common people looking at her.
Why not?
She's his only child. He does all he can to protect her.
From what?
From love.

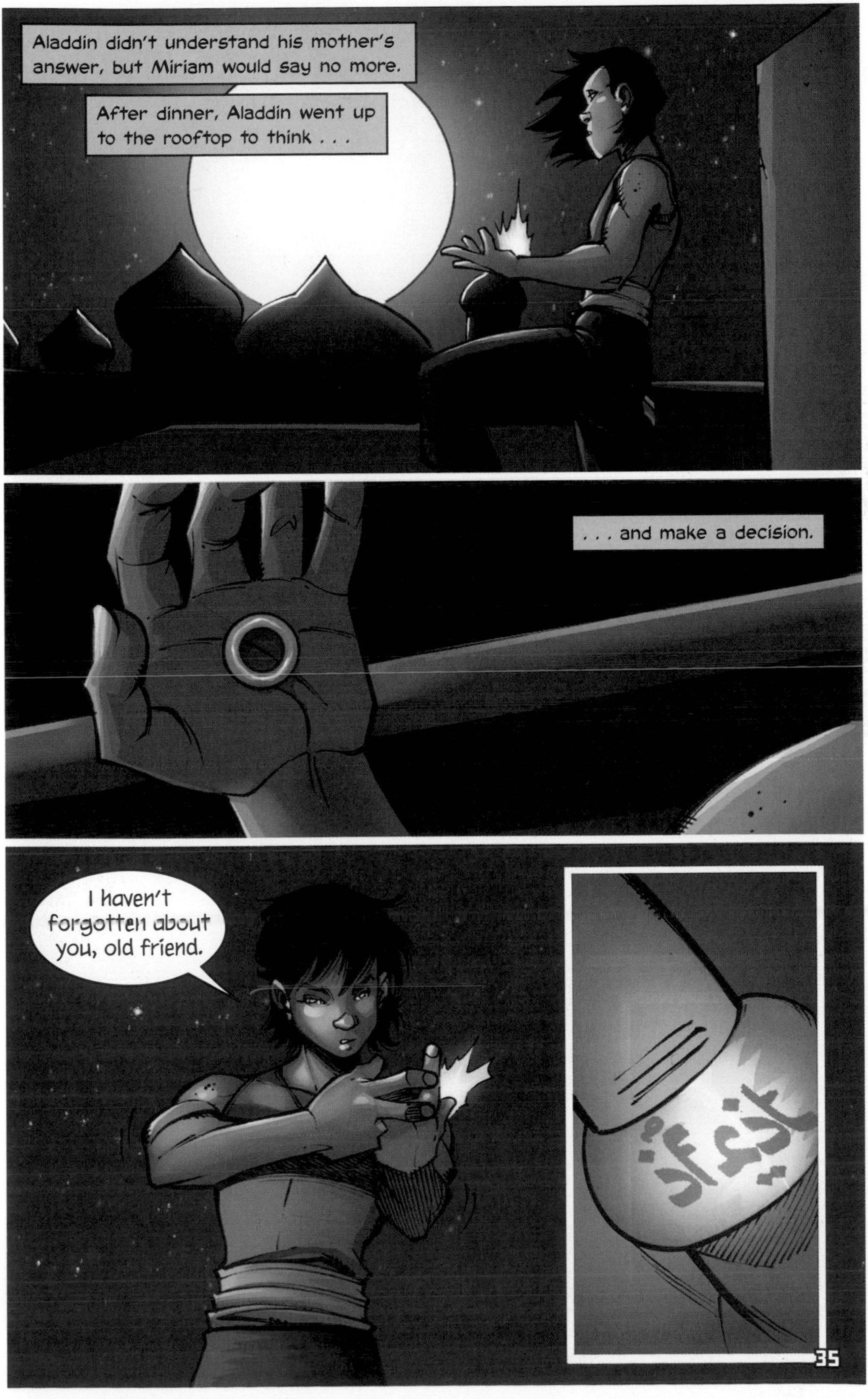
Aladdin didn't understand his mother's answer, but Miriam would say no more.
After dinner, Aladdin went up to the rooftop to think . . .
. . . and make a decision.
I haven't forgotten about you, old friend.

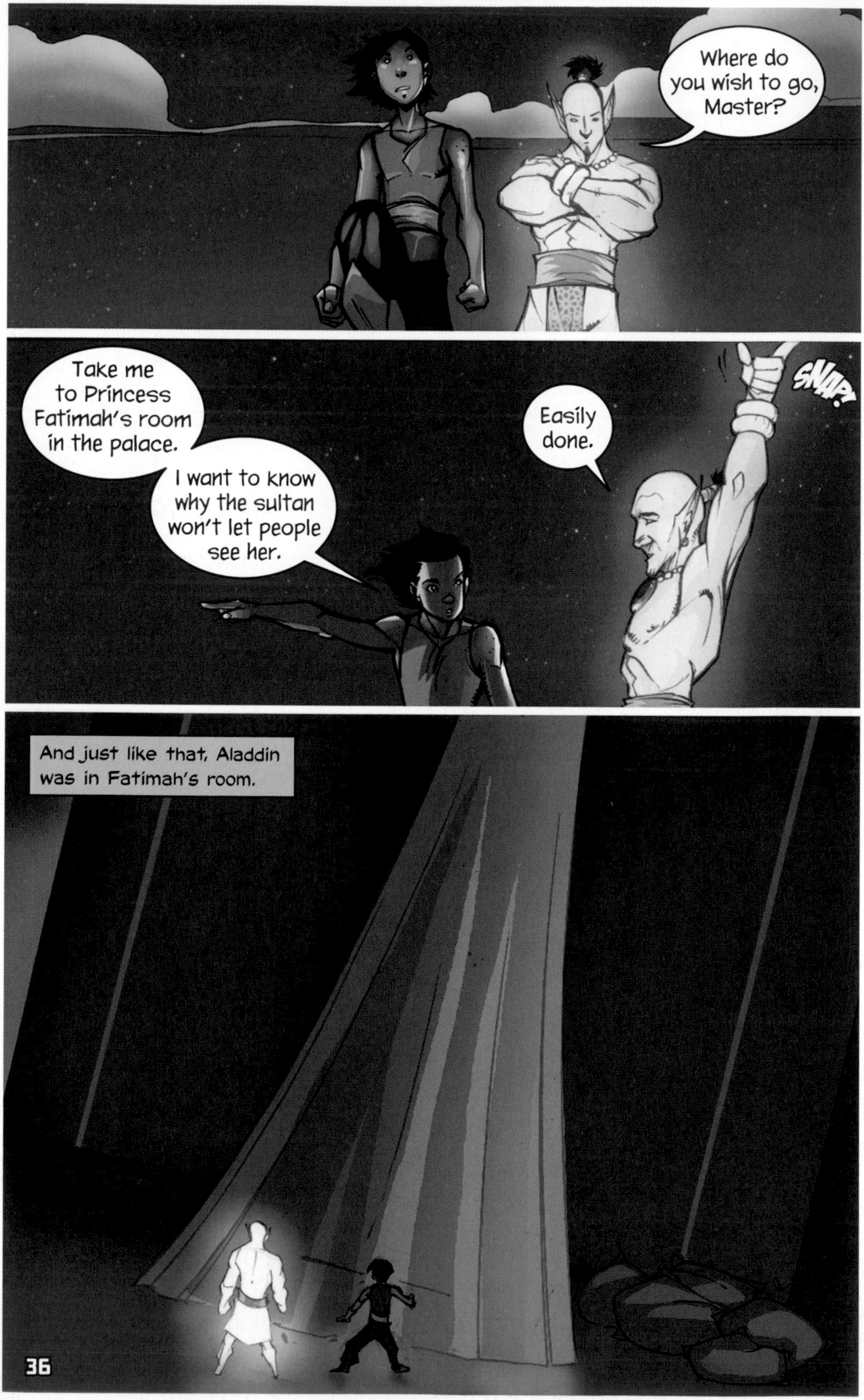
Where do you wish to go, Master?
Take me to Princess Fatimah's room in the palace.
I want to know why the sultan won't let people see her.
Easily done.
SNAP!
And just like that, Aladdin was in Fatimah's room.

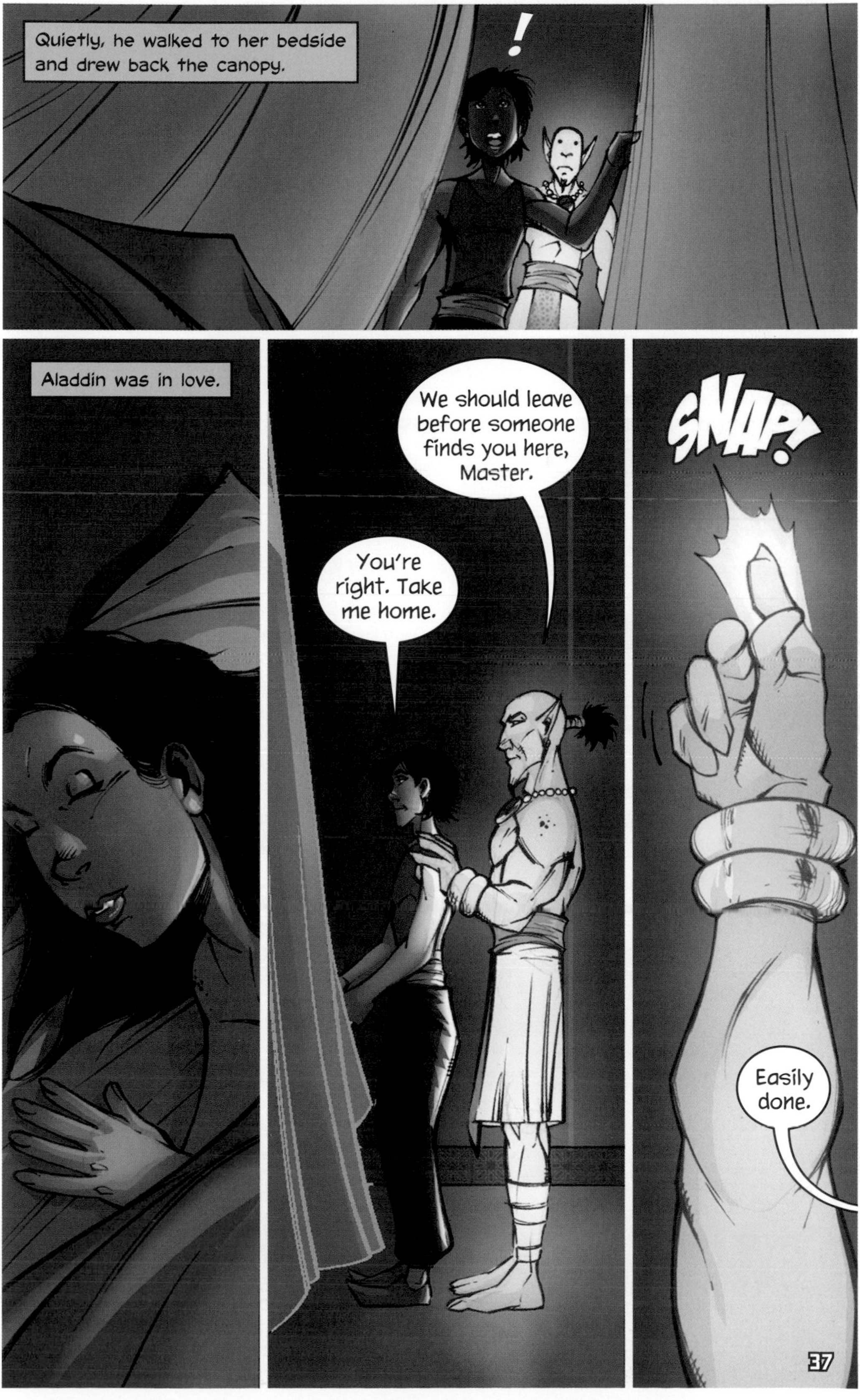
Quietly, he walked to her bedside and drew back the canopy.
!
Aladdin was in love.
We should leave before someone finds you here, Master.
You're right. Take me home.
SNAP!
Easily done.

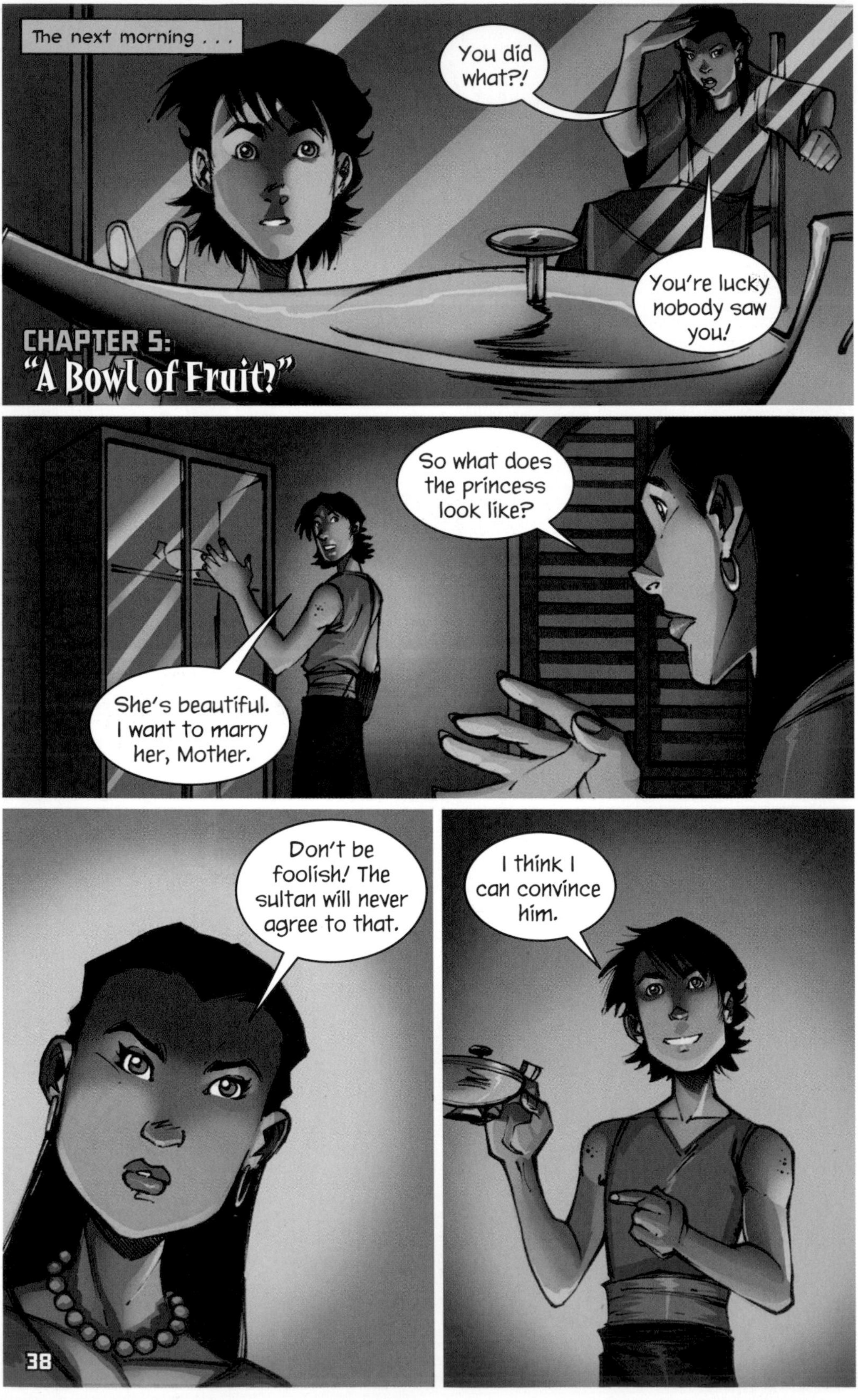
The next morning . . .
You did what?!
You're lucky nobody saw you!
CHAPTER 5:
"A Bowl of Fruit?"
So what does the princess look like?
She's beautiful. I want to marry her, Mother.
Don't be foolish! The sultan will never agree to that.
I think I can convince him.

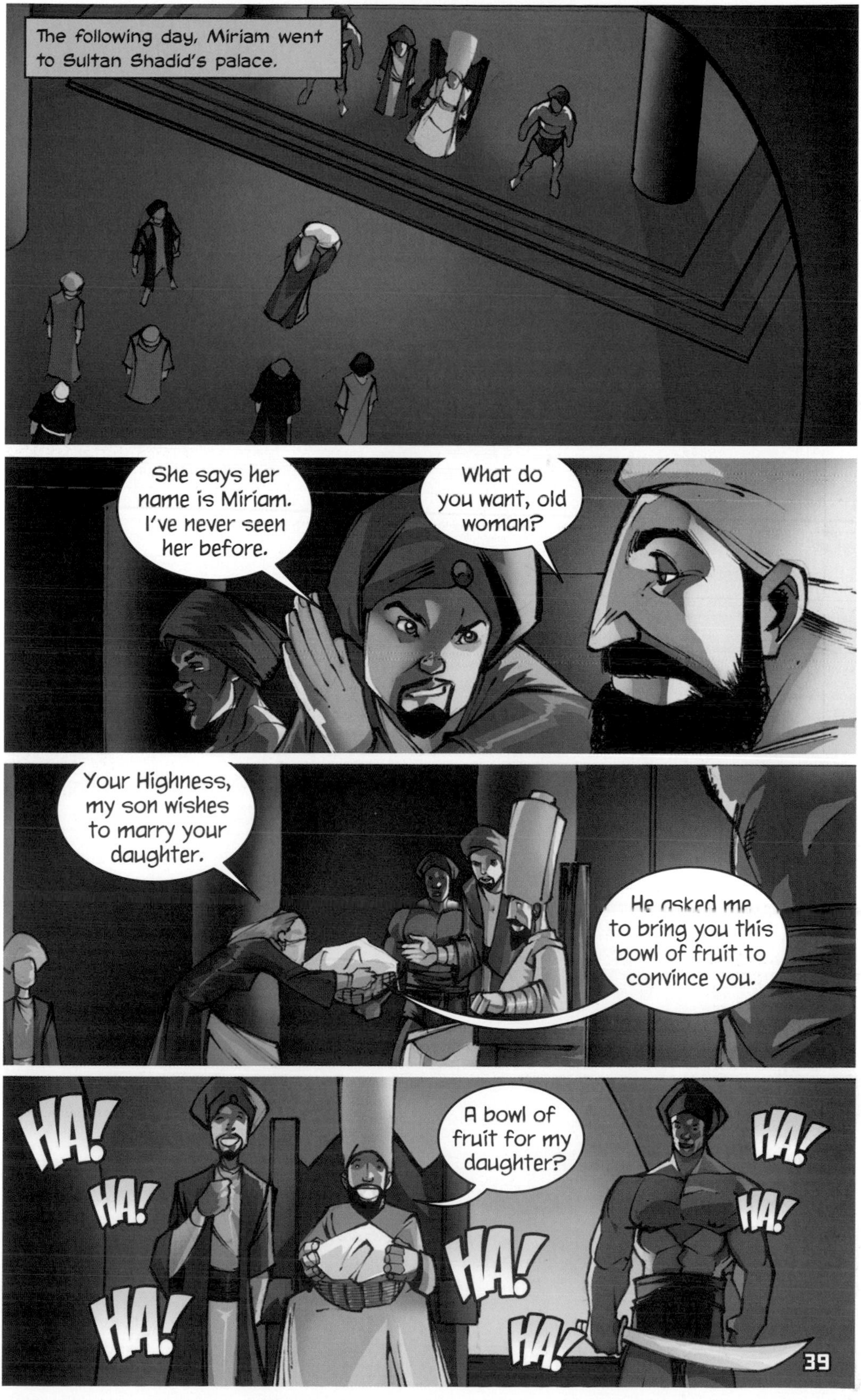
The following day, Miriam went to Sultan Shadid's palace.
She says her name is Miriam. I've never seen her before.
What do you want, old woman?
Your Highness, my son wishes to marry your daughter.
He asked me to bring you this bowl of fruit to convince you.
HA!
HA!
HA!
A bowl of fruit for my daughter?
HA!
HA!
HA!
HA!

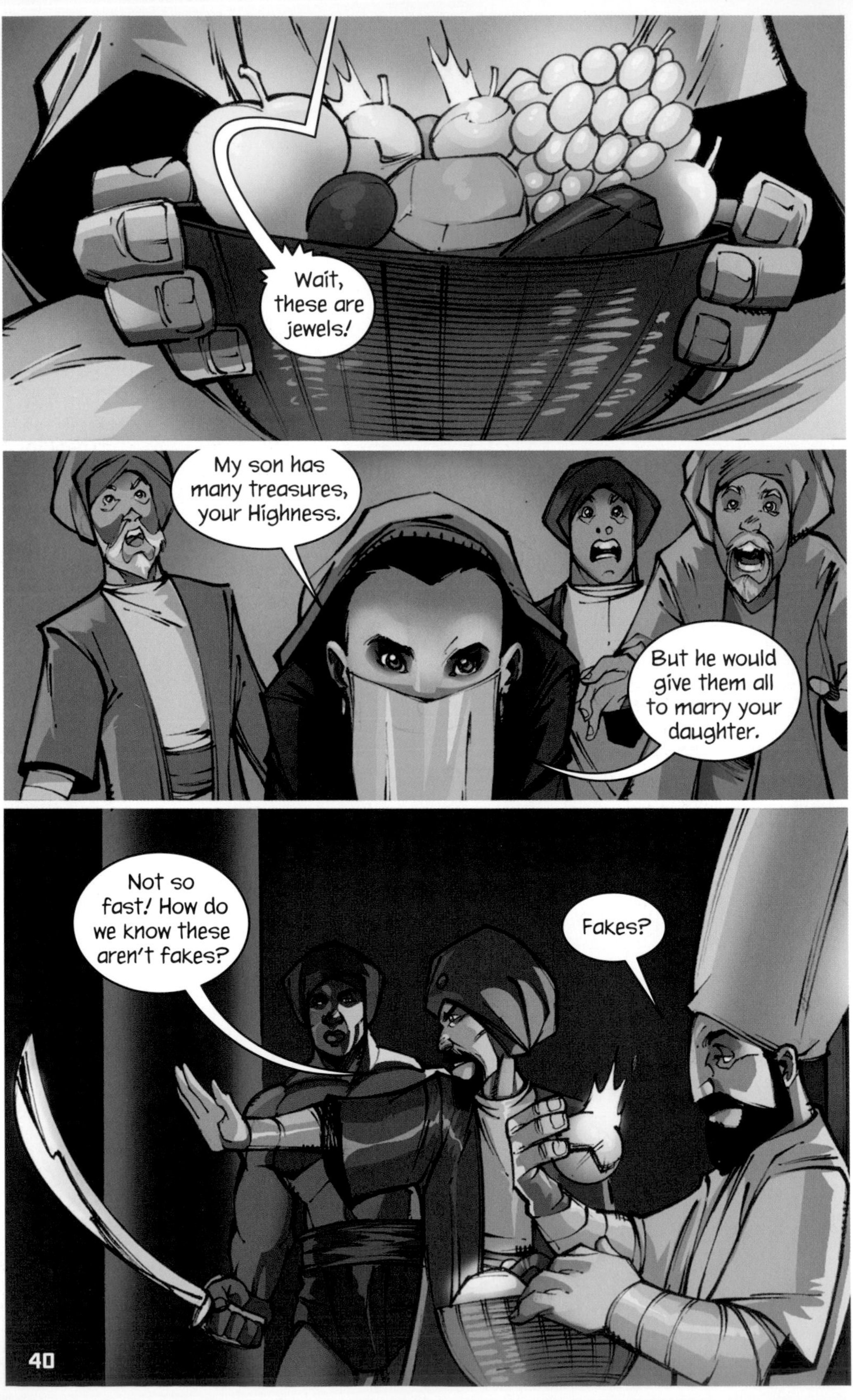
Wait, these are jewels!
My son has many treasures, your Highness.
But he would give them all to marry your daughter.
Not so fast! How do we know these aren't fakes?
Fakes?

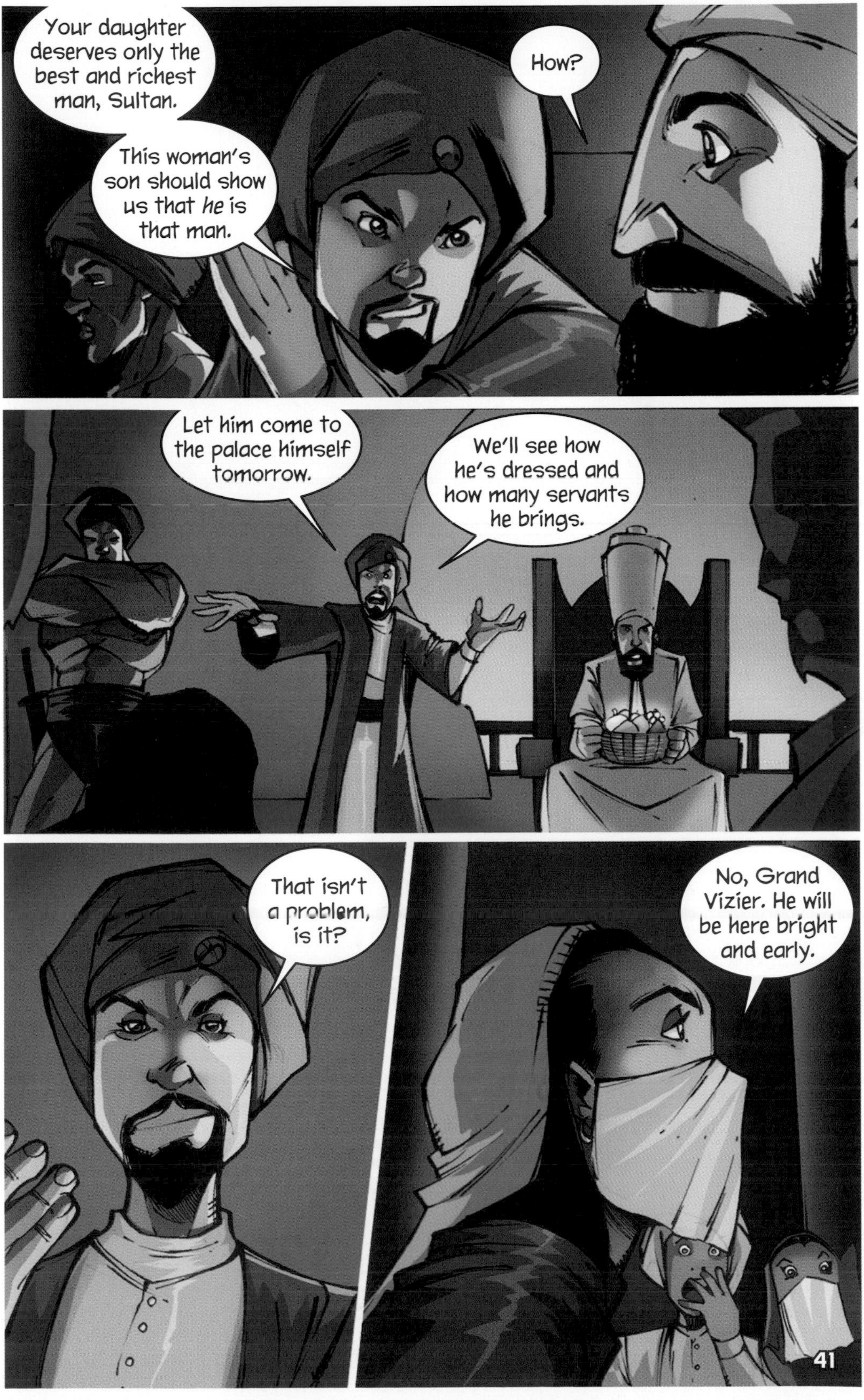
Your daughter deserves only the best and richest man, Sultan.
This woman's son should show us that *he* is that man.
How?
Let him come to the palace himself tomorrow.
We'll see how he's dressed and how many servants he brings.
That isn't a problem, is it?
No, Grand Vizier. He will be here bright and early.

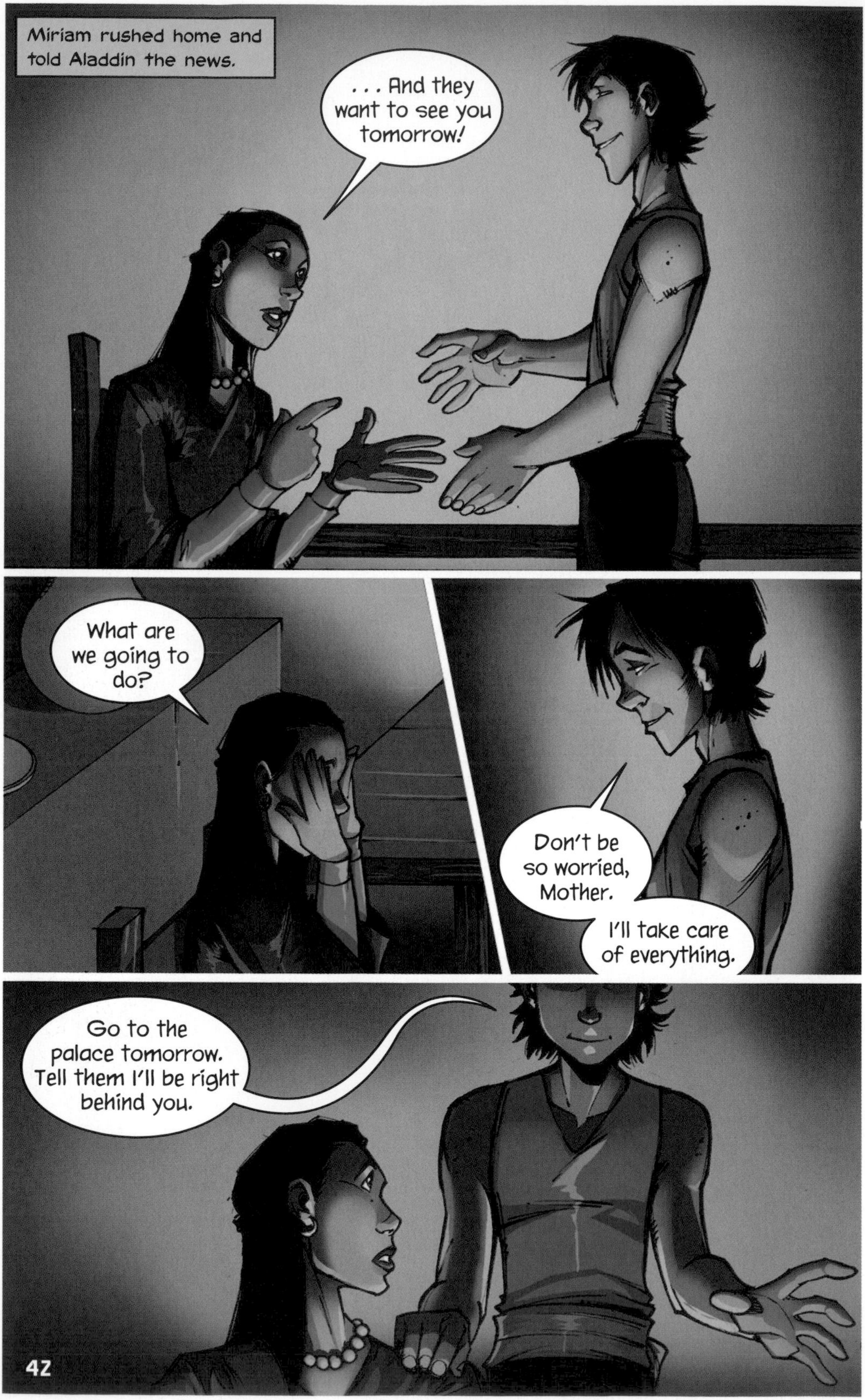
Miriam rushed home and told Aladdin the news.
. . . And they want to see you tomorrow!
What are we going to do?
Don't be so worried, Mother.
I'll take care of everything.
Go to the palace tomorrow. Tell them I'll be right behind you.

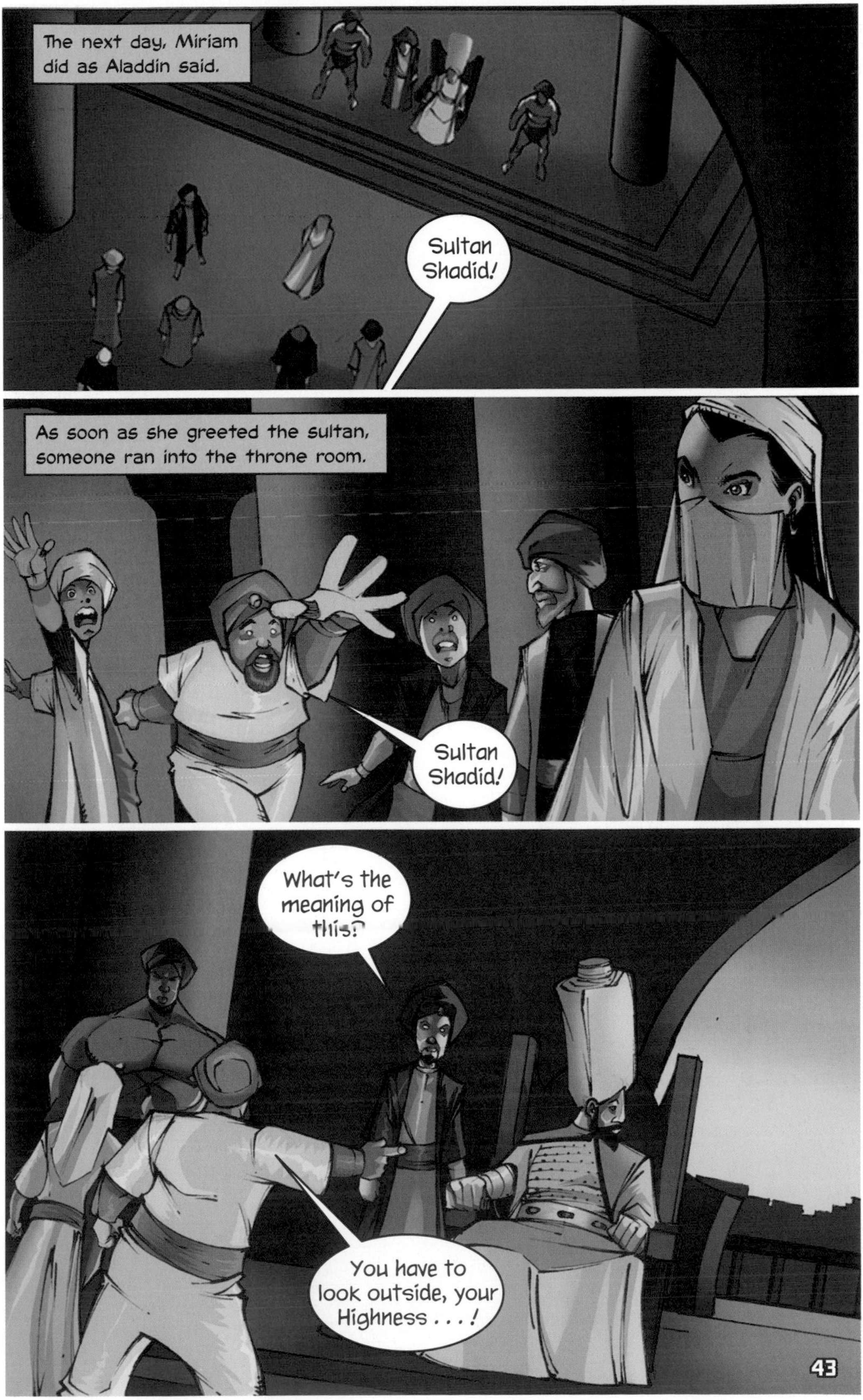
The next day, Miriam did as Aladdin said.
Sultan Shadid!
As soon as she greeted the sultan, someone ran into the throne room.
Sultan Shadid!
What's the meaning of this?
You have to look outside, your Highness . . . !

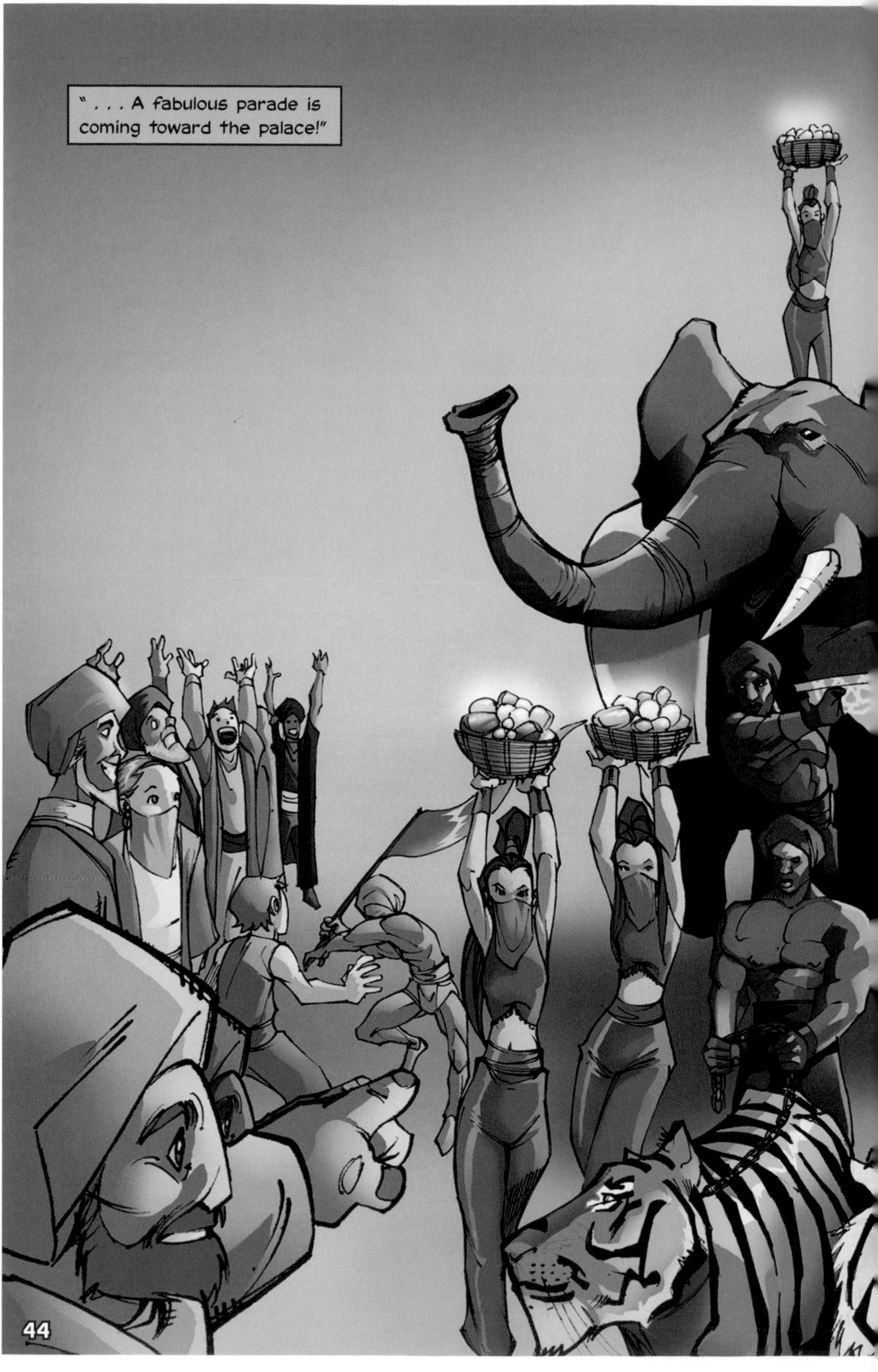
". . . A fabulous parade is coming toward the palace!"

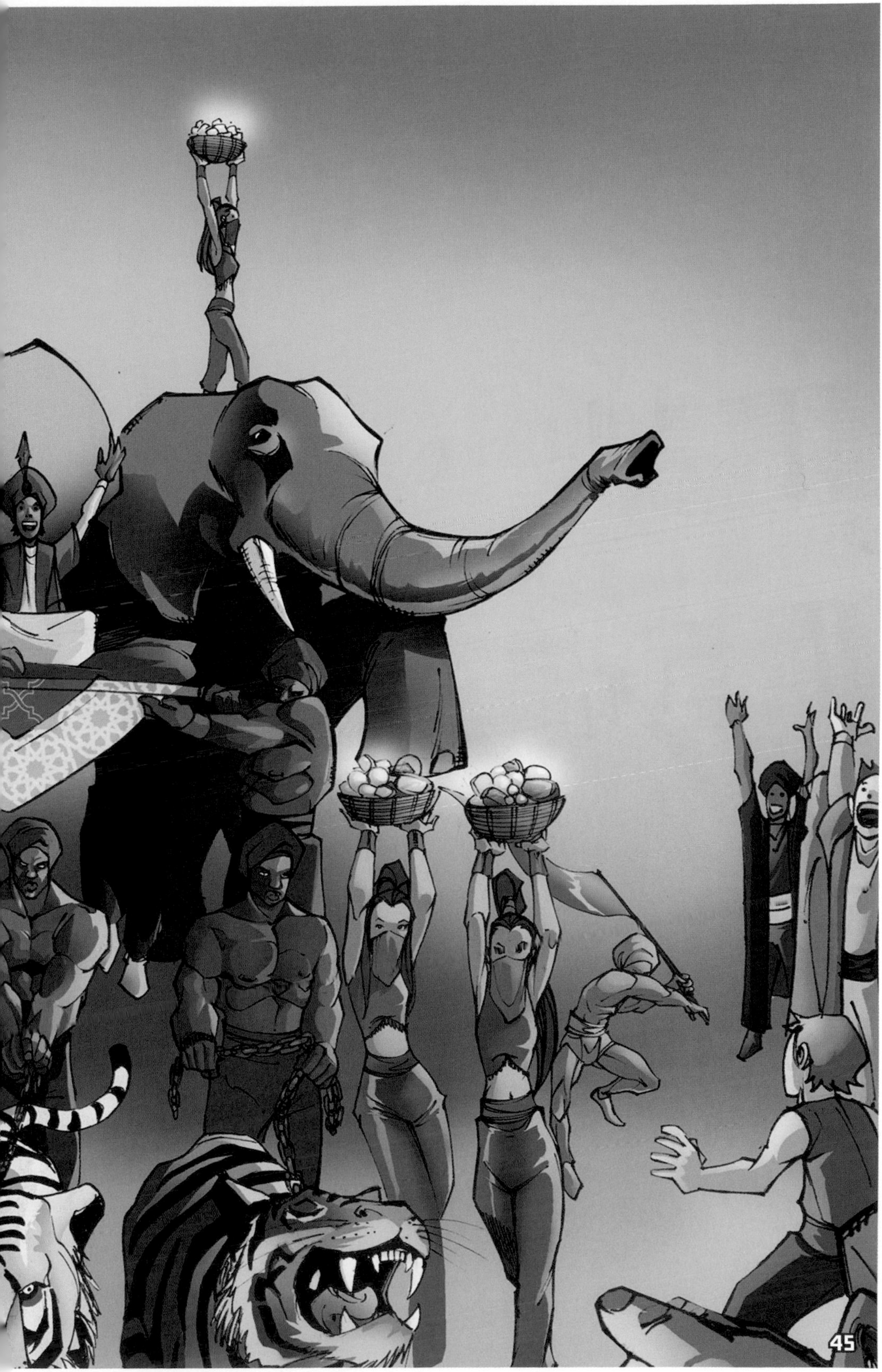

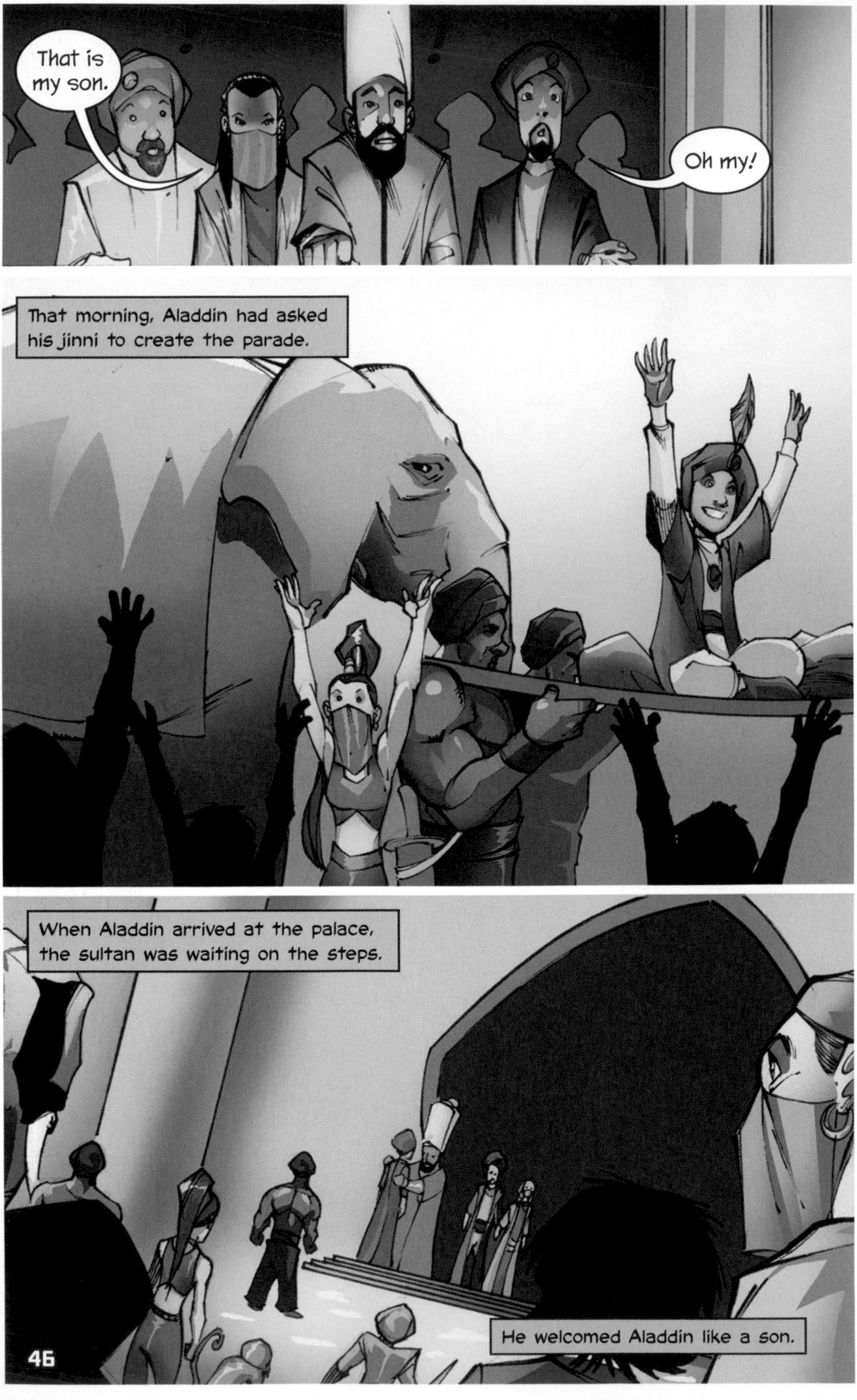
That is my son.
Oh my!
That morning, Aladdin had asked his jinni to create the parade.
When Aladdin arrived at the palace, the sultan was waiting on the steps.
He welcomed Aladdin like a son.

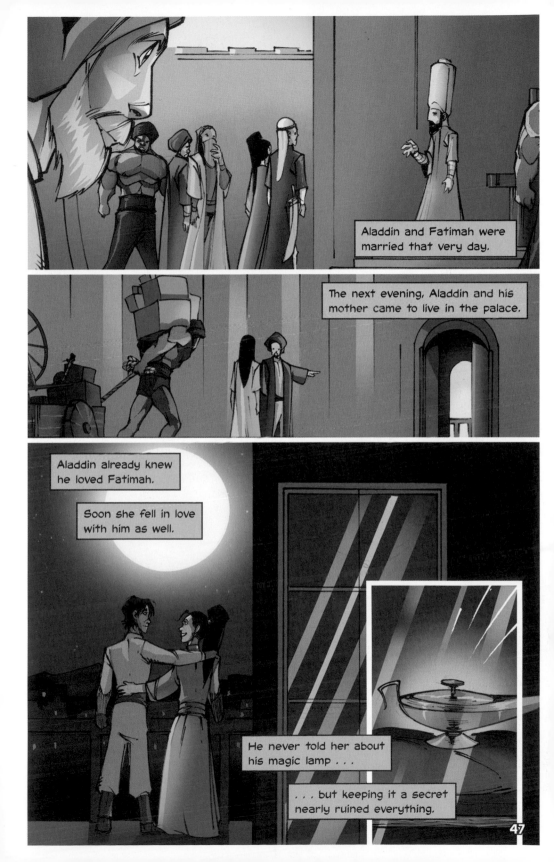

Aladdin and Fatimah were married that very day.

The next evening, Aladdin and his mother came to live in the palace.

Aladdin already knew he loved Fatimah.

Soon she fell in love with him as well.

He never told her about his magic lamp . . .

. . . but keeping it a secret nearly ruined everything.

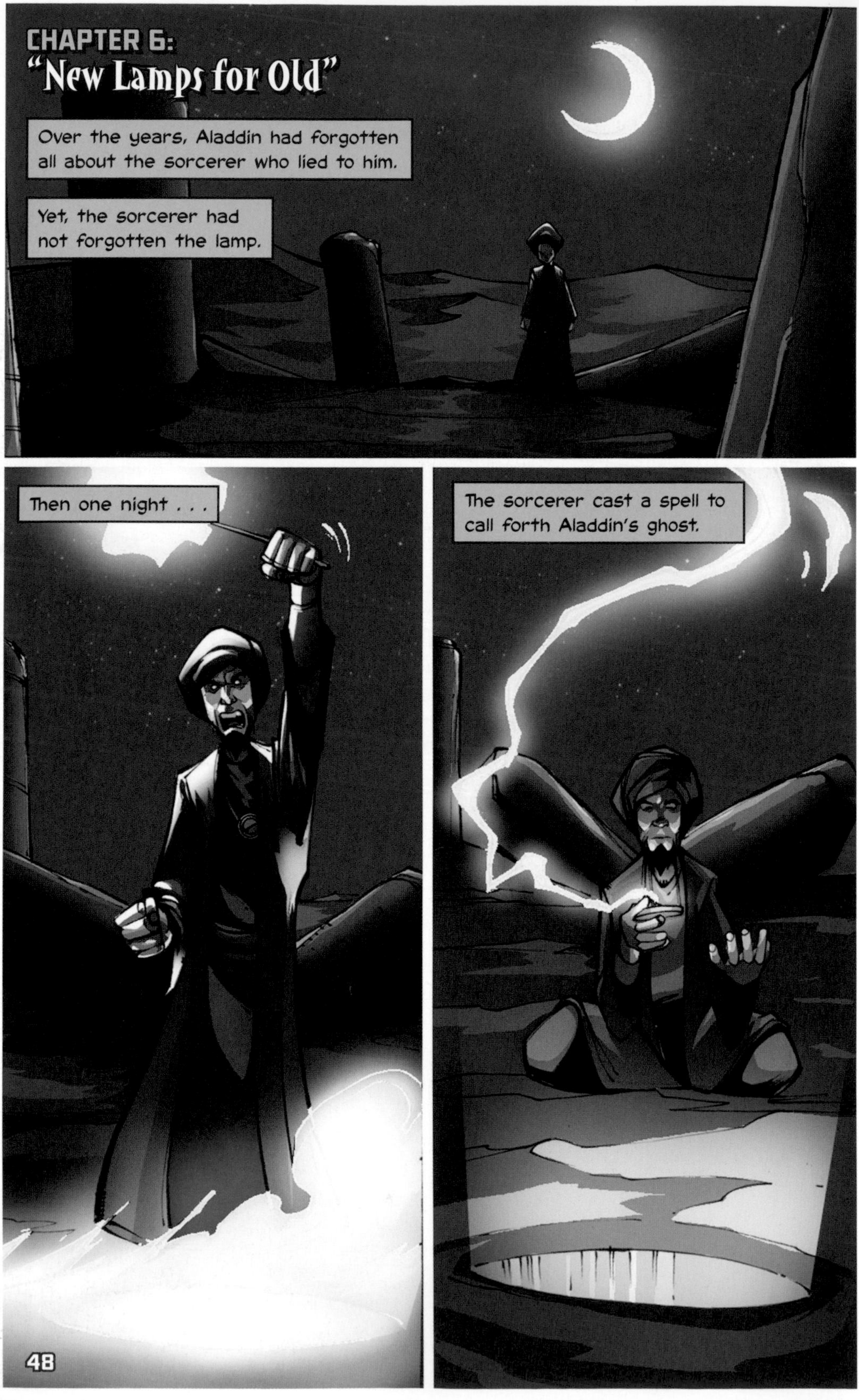
CHAPTER 6:
"New Lamps for Old"
Over the years, Aladdin had forgotten all about the sorcerer who lied to him.
Yet, the sorcerer had not forgotten the lamp.
Then one night . . .
The sorcerer cast a spell to call forth Aladdin's ghost.

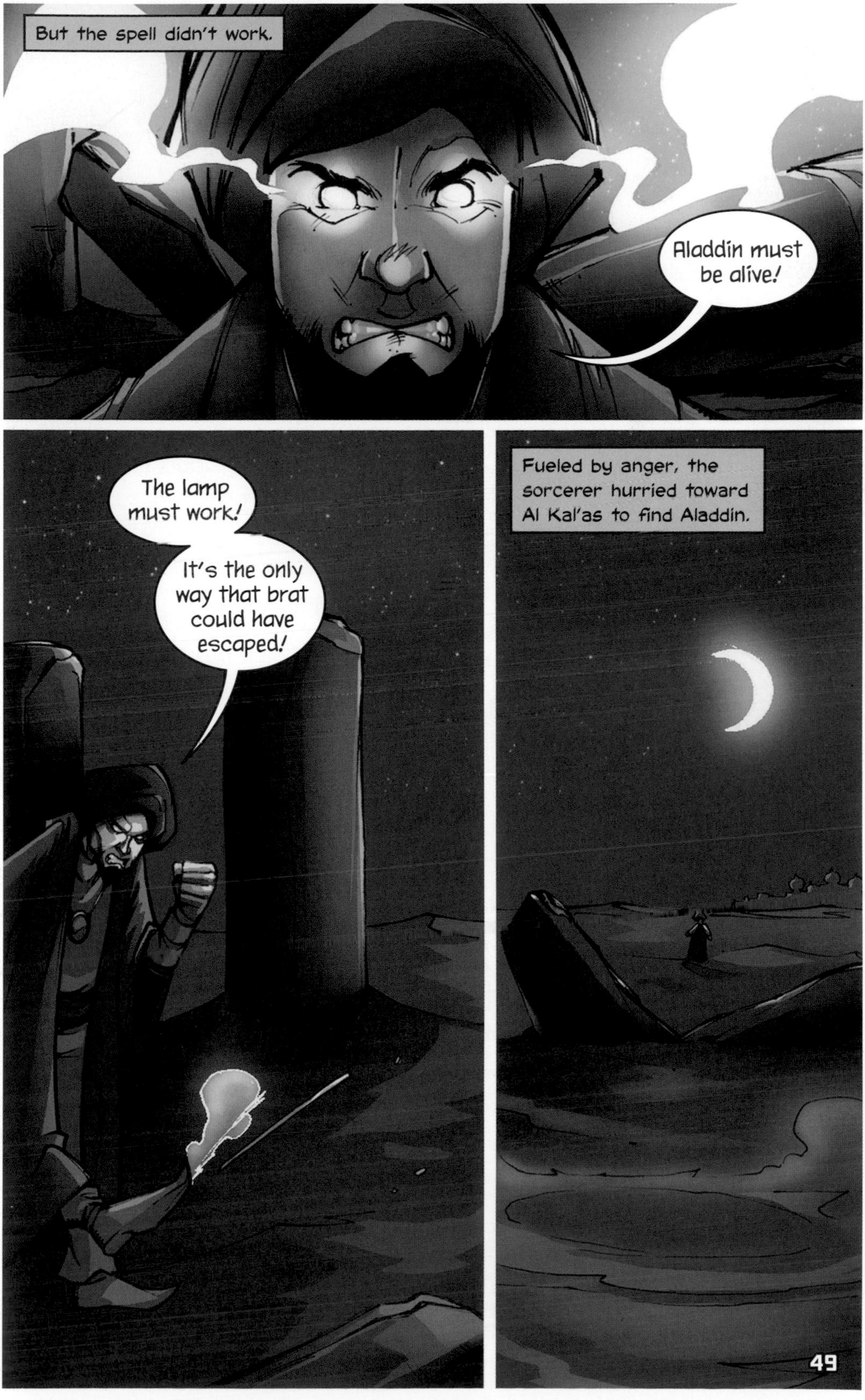
But the spell didn't work.
Aladdin must be alive!
The lamp must work!
It's the only way that brat could have escaped!
Fueled by anger, the sorcerer hurried toward Al Kal'as to find Aladdin.

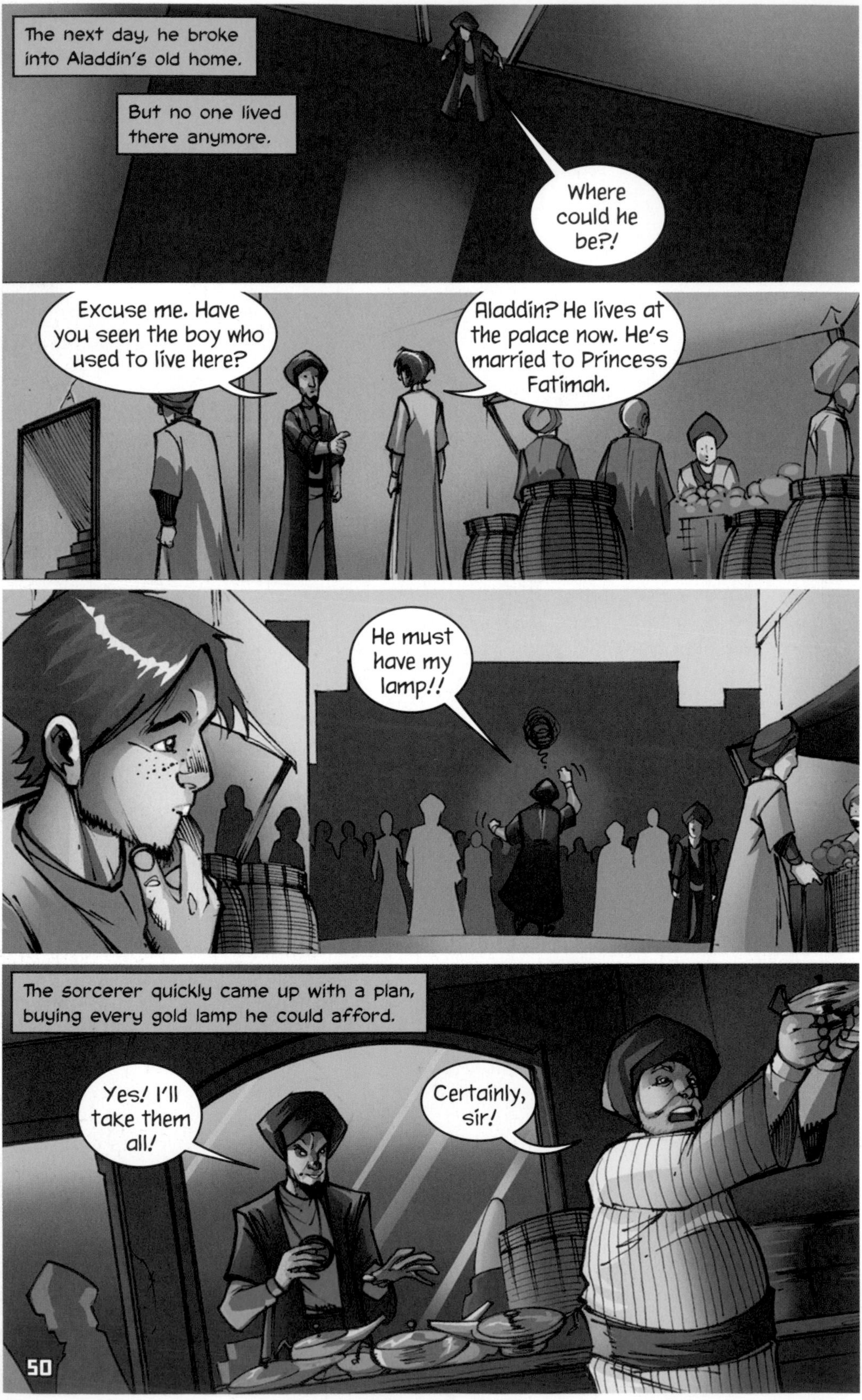
The next day, he broke into Aladdin's old home.
But no one lived there anymore.
Where could he be?!
Excuse me. Have you seen the boy who used to live here?
Aladdin? He lives at the palace now. He's married to Princess Fatimah.
He must have my lamp!!
The sorcerer quickly came up with a plan, buying every gold lamp he could afford.
Yes! I'll take them all!
Certainly, sir!

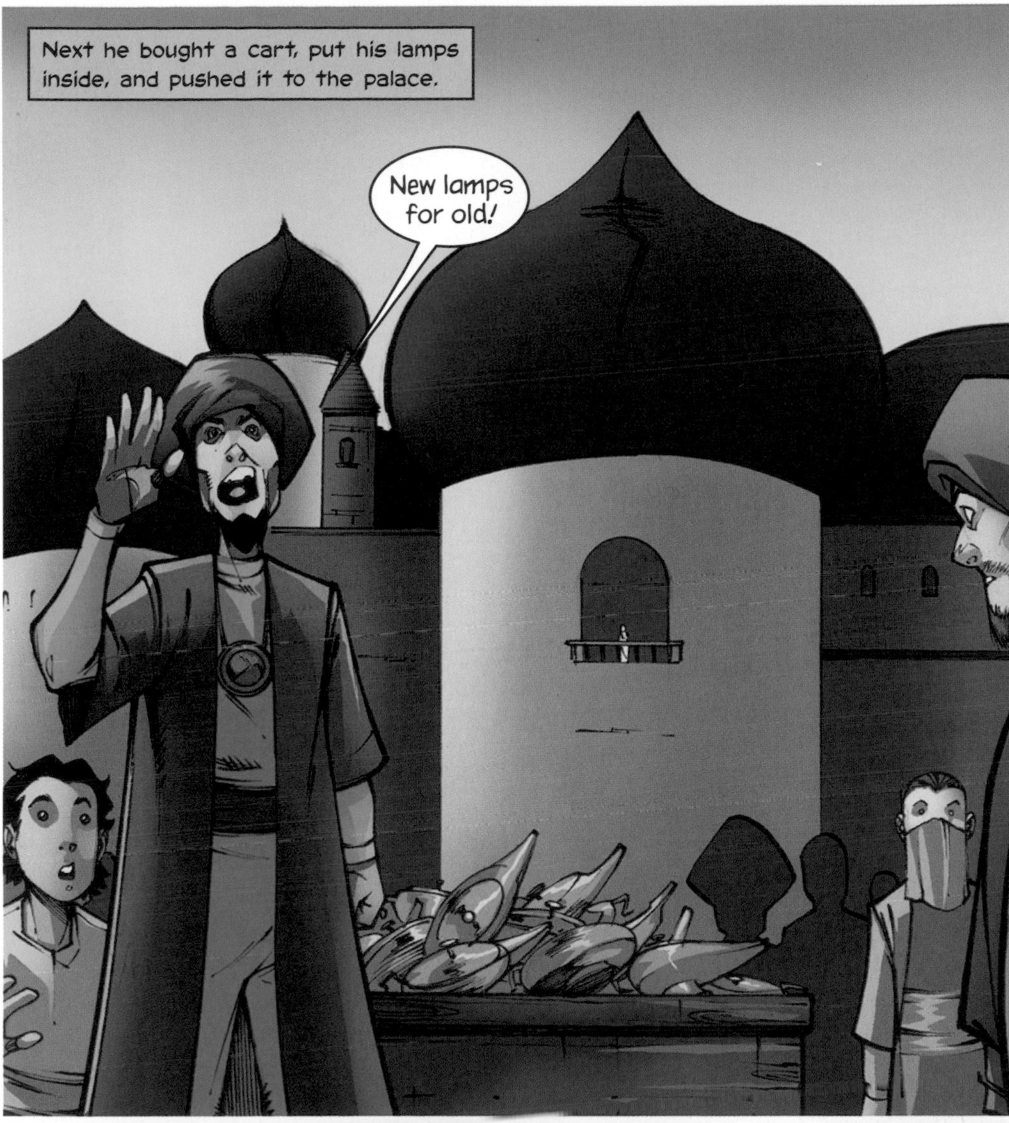
Next he bought a cart, put his lamps inside, and pushed it to the palace.
New lamps for old!

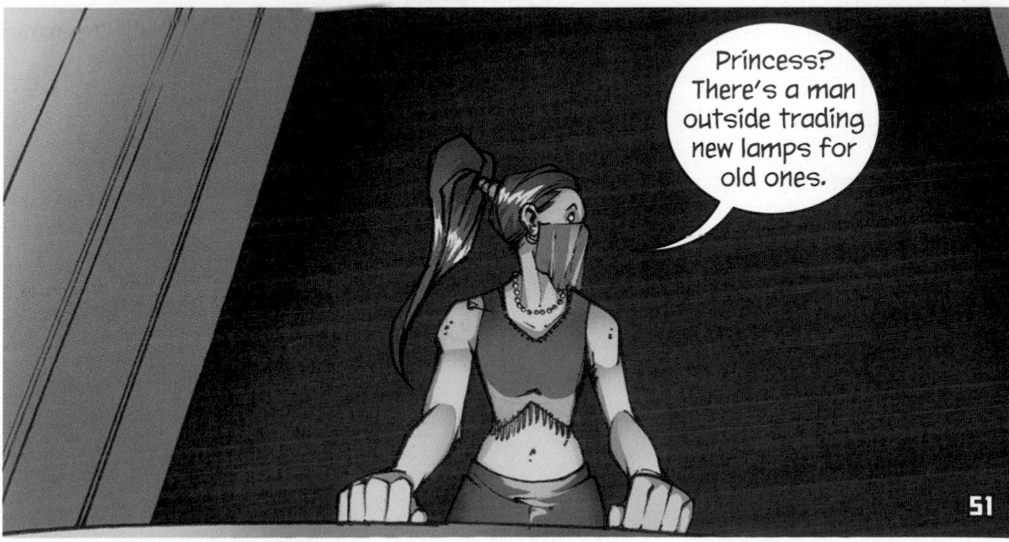
Princess? There's a man outside trading new lamps for old ones.

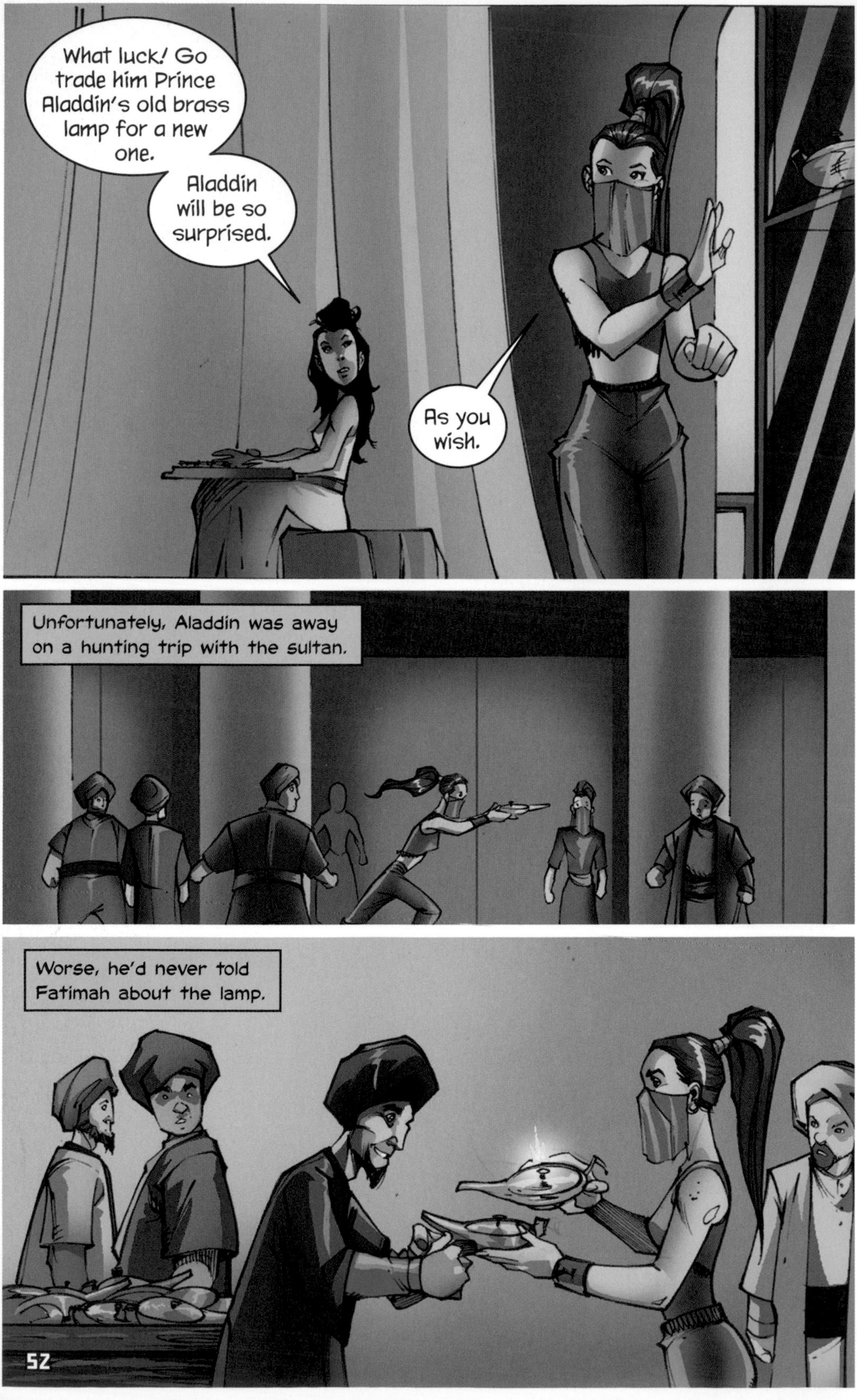
What luck! Go trade him Prince Aladdin's old brass lamp for a new one.
Aladdin will be so surprised.
As you wish.
Unfortunately, Aladdin was away on a hunting trip with the sultan.
Worse, he'd never told Fatimah about the lamp.

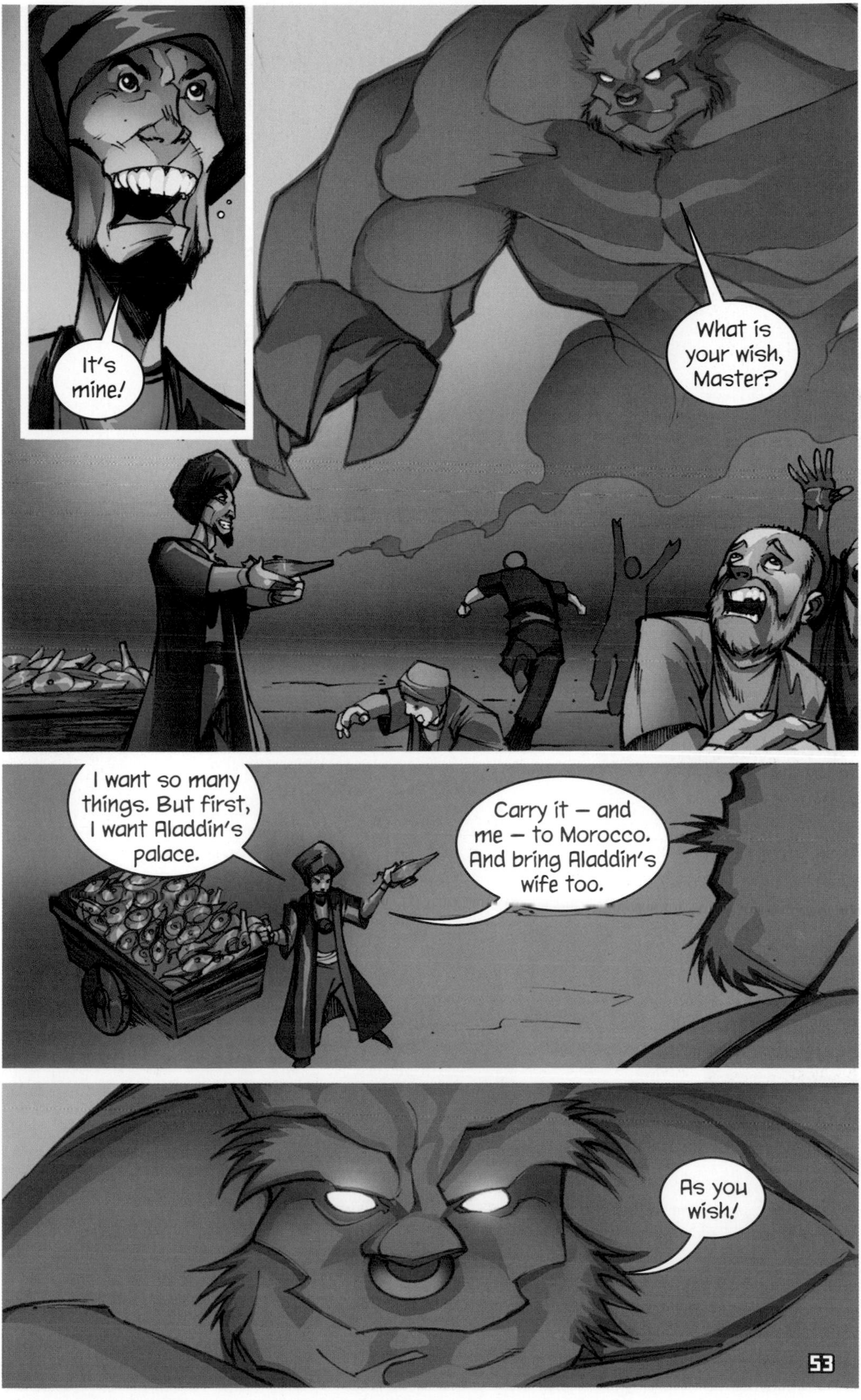
It's mine!
What is your wish, Master?
I want so many things. But first, I want Aladdin's palace.
Carry it — and me — to Morocco. And bring Aladdin's wife too.
As you wish!

CHAPTER 7: "You've Had Your Fun!"

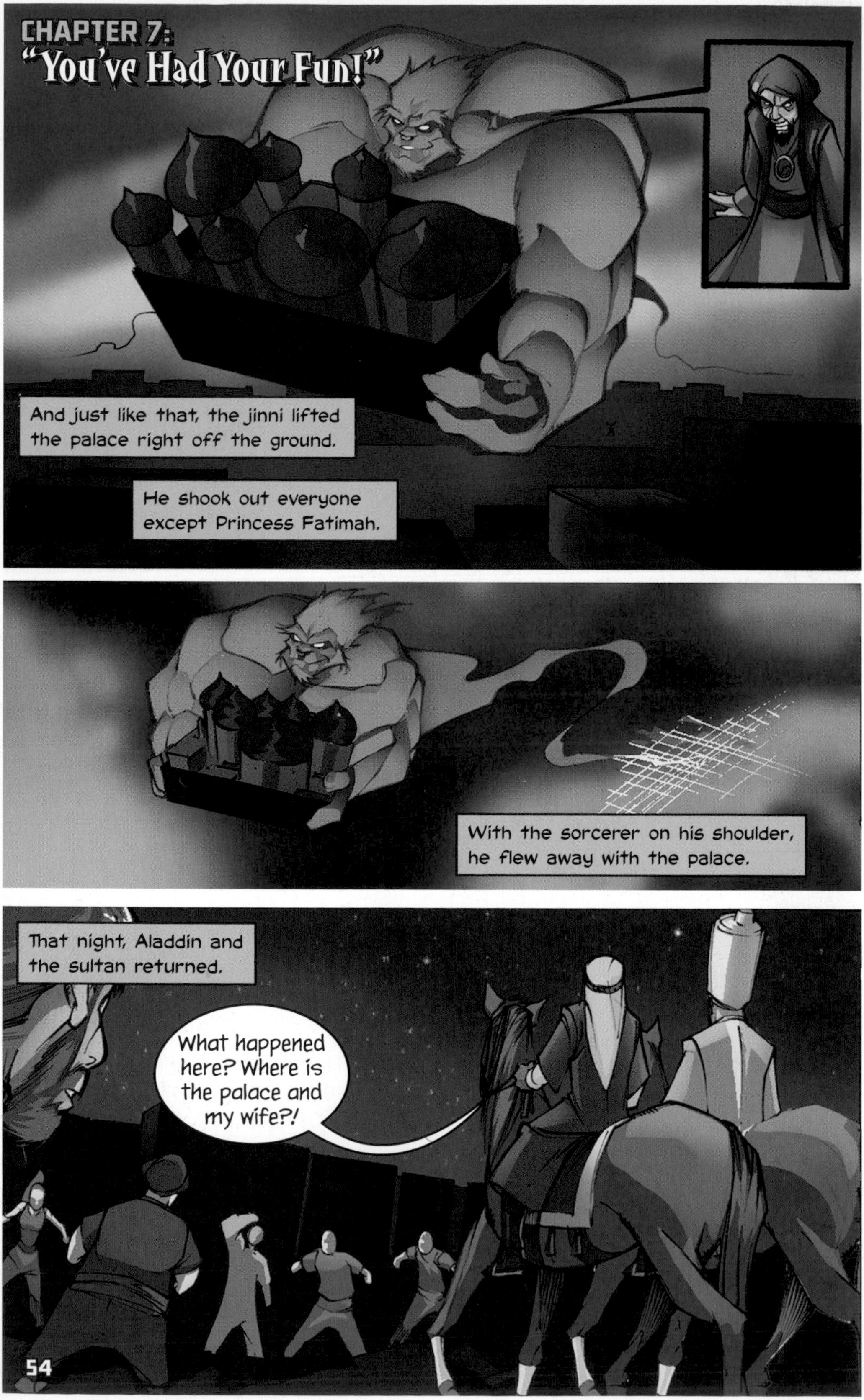

And just like that, the jinni lifted the palace right off the ground.
He shook out everyone except Princess Fatimah.
With the sorcerer on his shoulder, he flew away with the palace.
That night, Aladdin and the sultan returned.
What happened here? Where is the palace and my wife?!

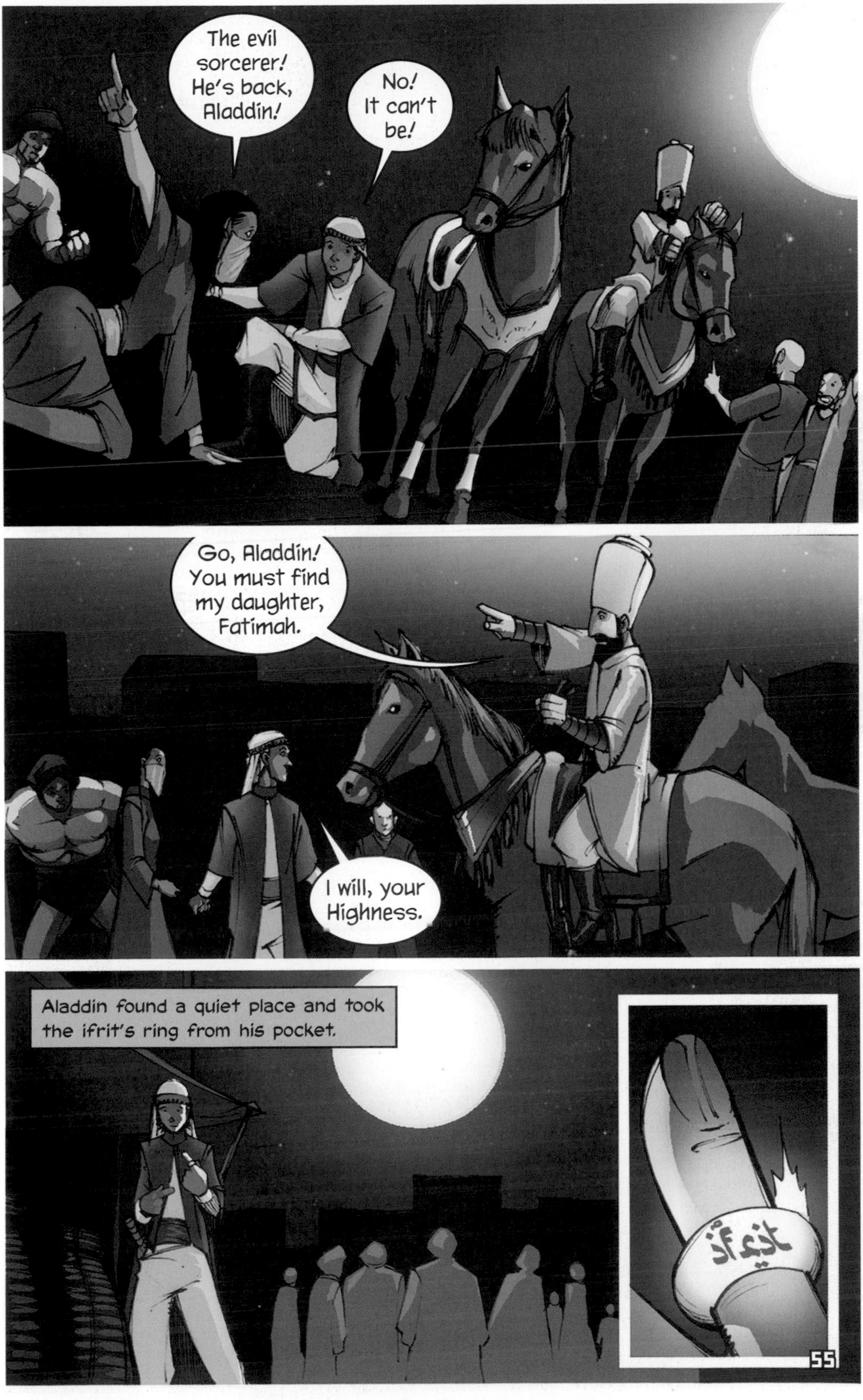
The evil sorcerer! He's back, Aladdin!
No! It can't be!
Go, Aladdin! You must find my daughter, Fatimah.
I will, your Highness.
Aladdin found a quiet place and took the ifrit's ring from his pocket.
ifrit

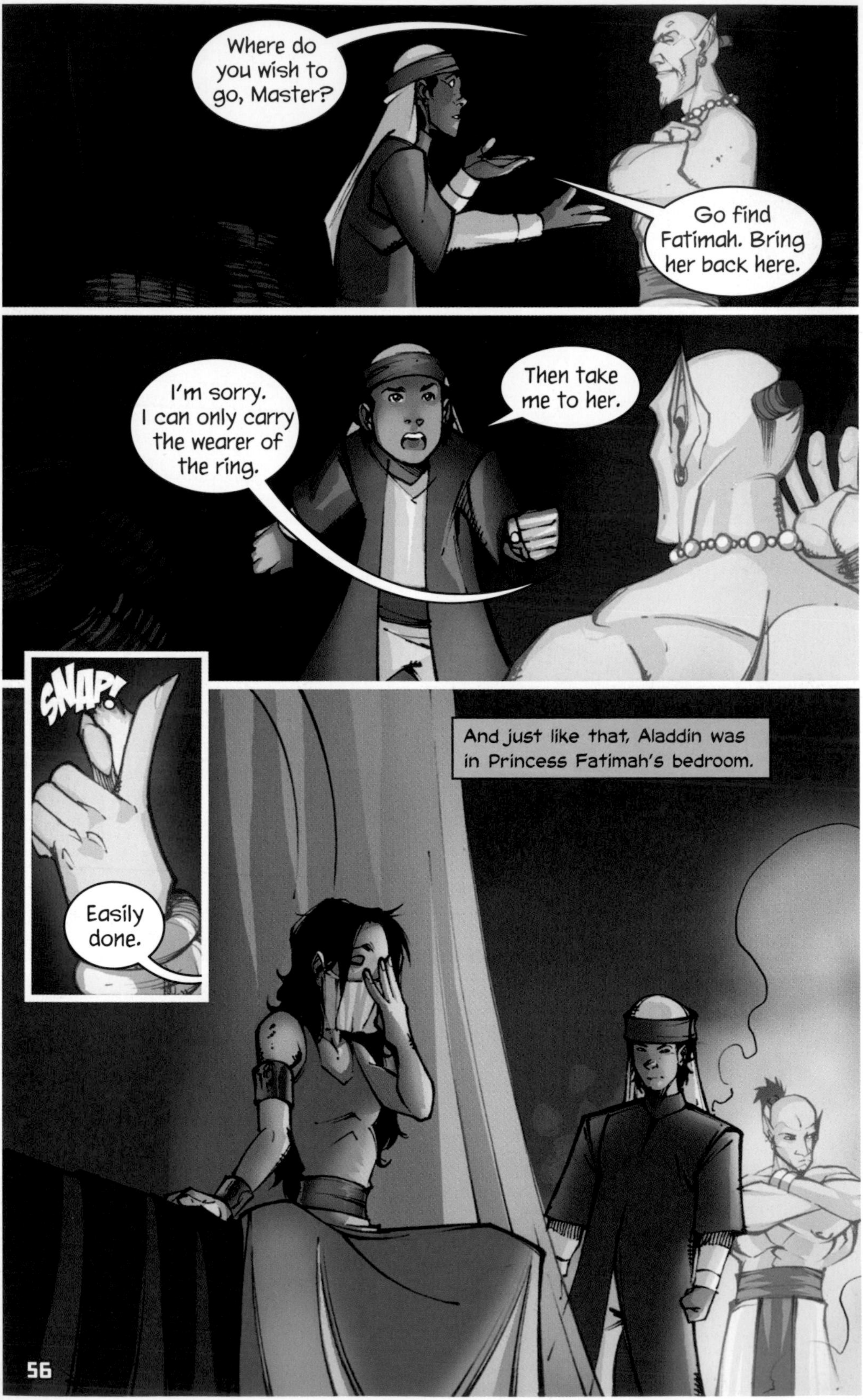
Where do you wish to go, Master?
Go find Fatimah. Bring her back here.
I'm sorry. I can only carry the wearer of the ring.
Then take me to her.
SNAP!
Easily done.
And just like that, Aladdin was in Princess Fatimah's bedroom.

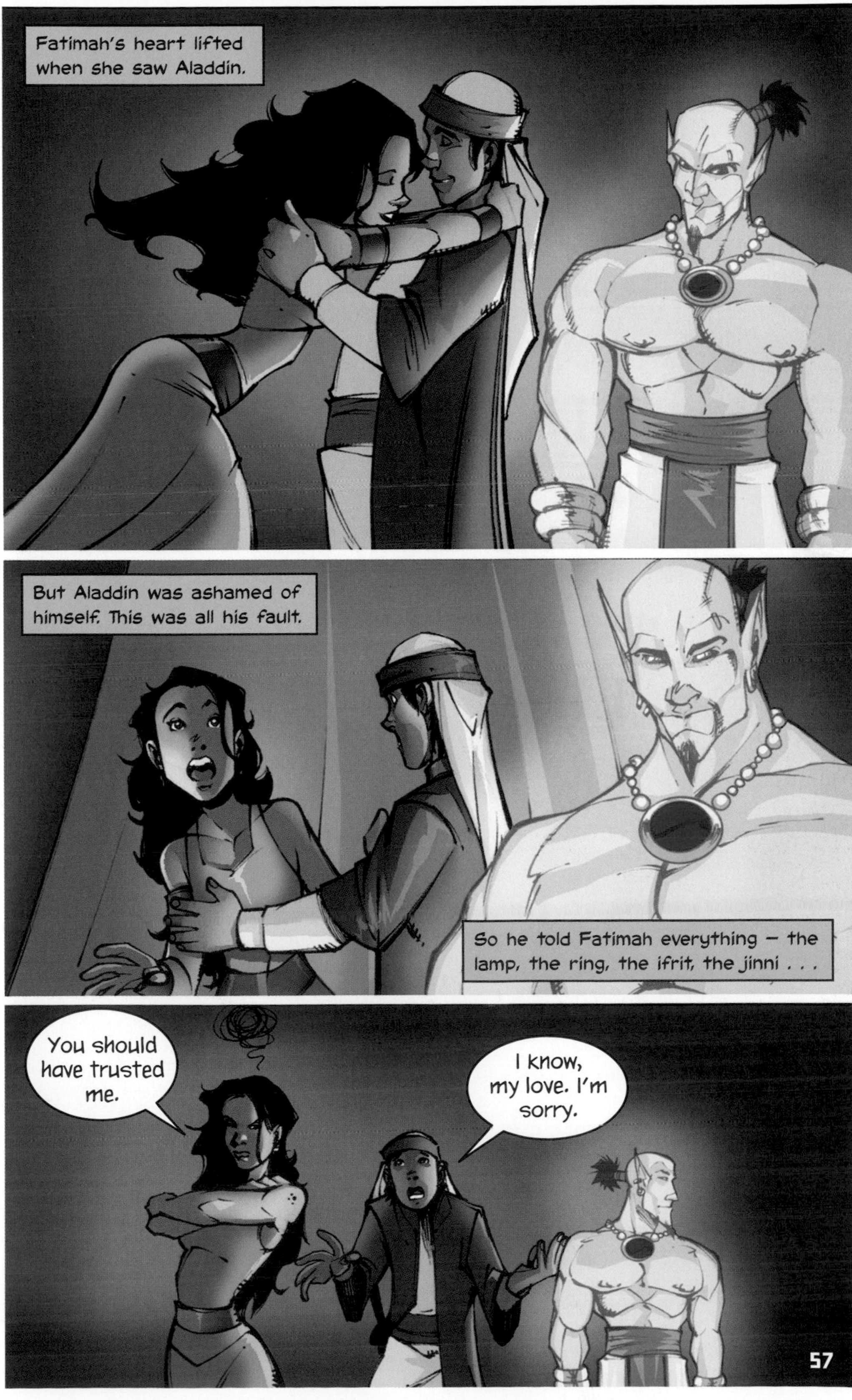

Fatimah's heart lifted when she saw Aladdin.
But Aladdin was ashamed of himself. This was all his fault.
So he told Fatimah everything — the lamp, the ring, the ifrit, the jinni . . .
You should have trusted me.
I know, my love. I'm sorry.

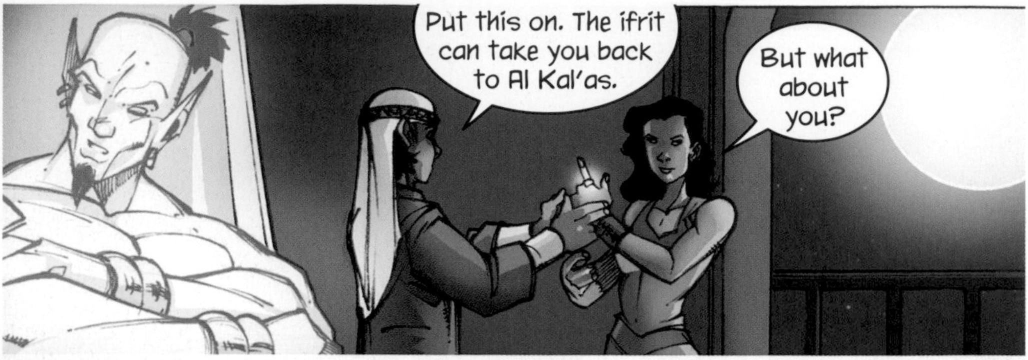
Put this on. The ifrit can take you back to Al Kal'as.
But what about you?

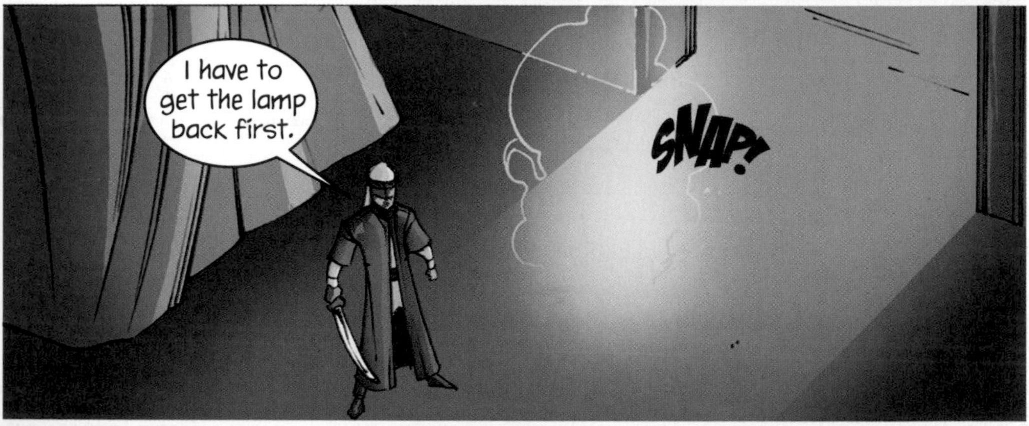
I have to get the lamp back first.
SNAP!

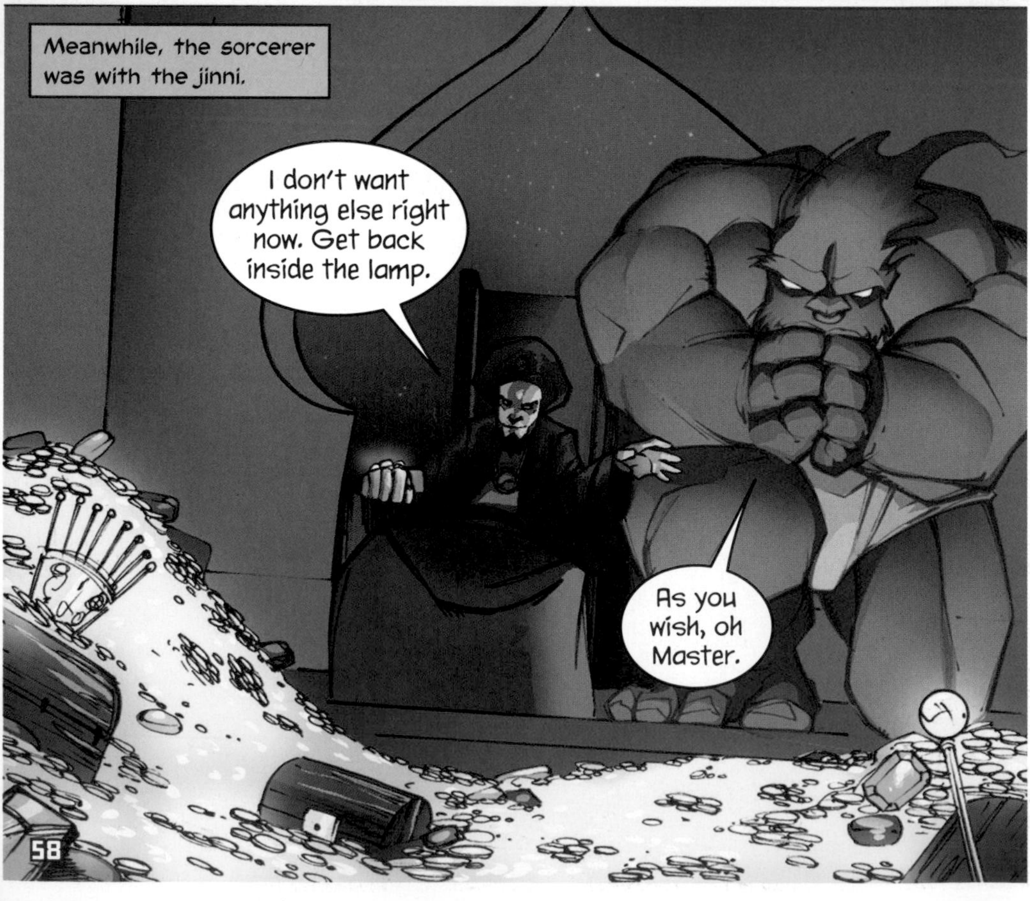
Meanwhile, the sorcerer was with the jinni.
I don't want anything else right now. Get back inside the lamp.
As you wish, oh Master.

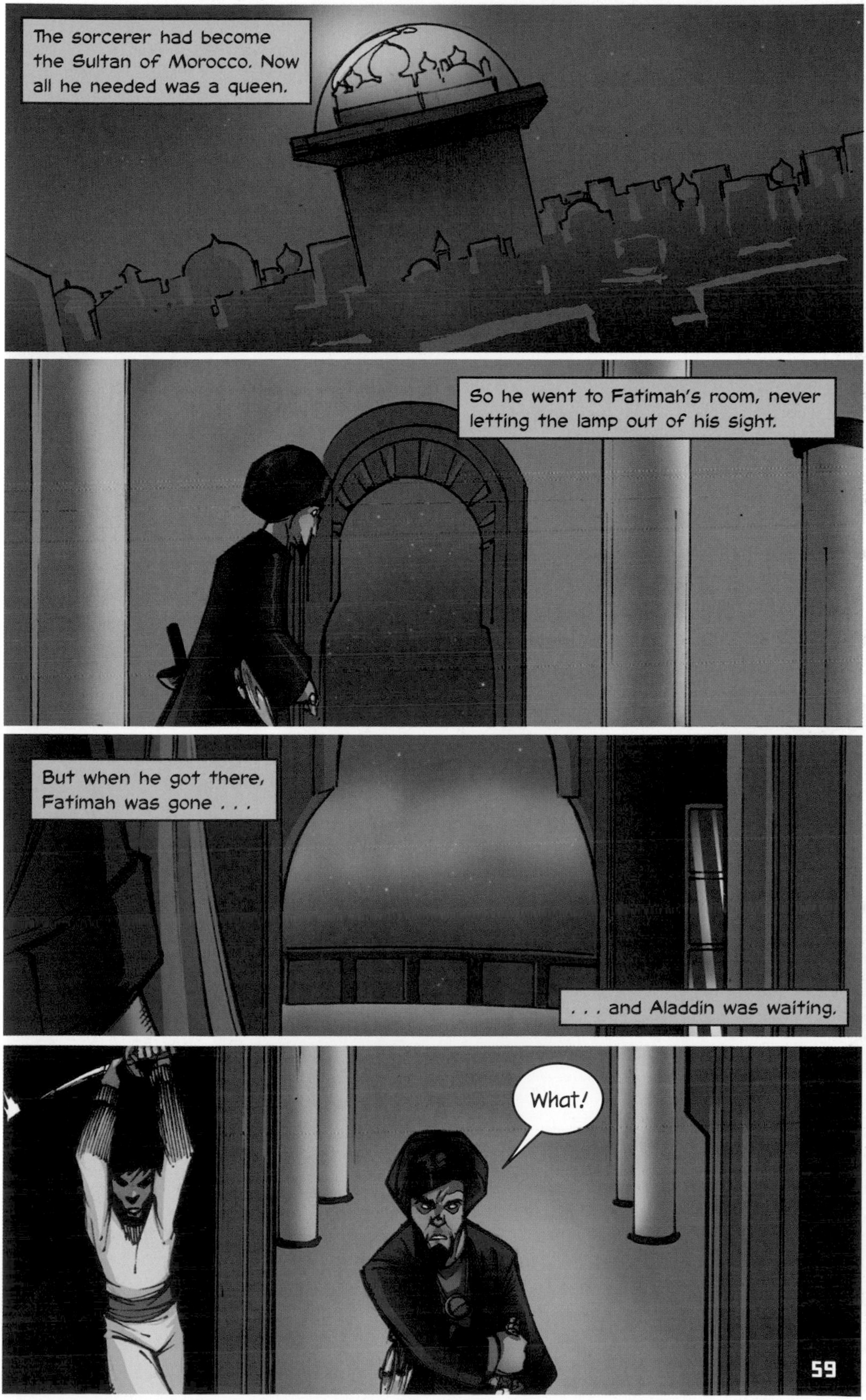
The sorcerer had become the Sultan of Morocco. Now all he needed was a queen.
So he went to Fatimah's room, never letting the lamp out of his sight.
But when he got there, Fatimah was gone . . .
. . . and Aladdin was waiting.
What!

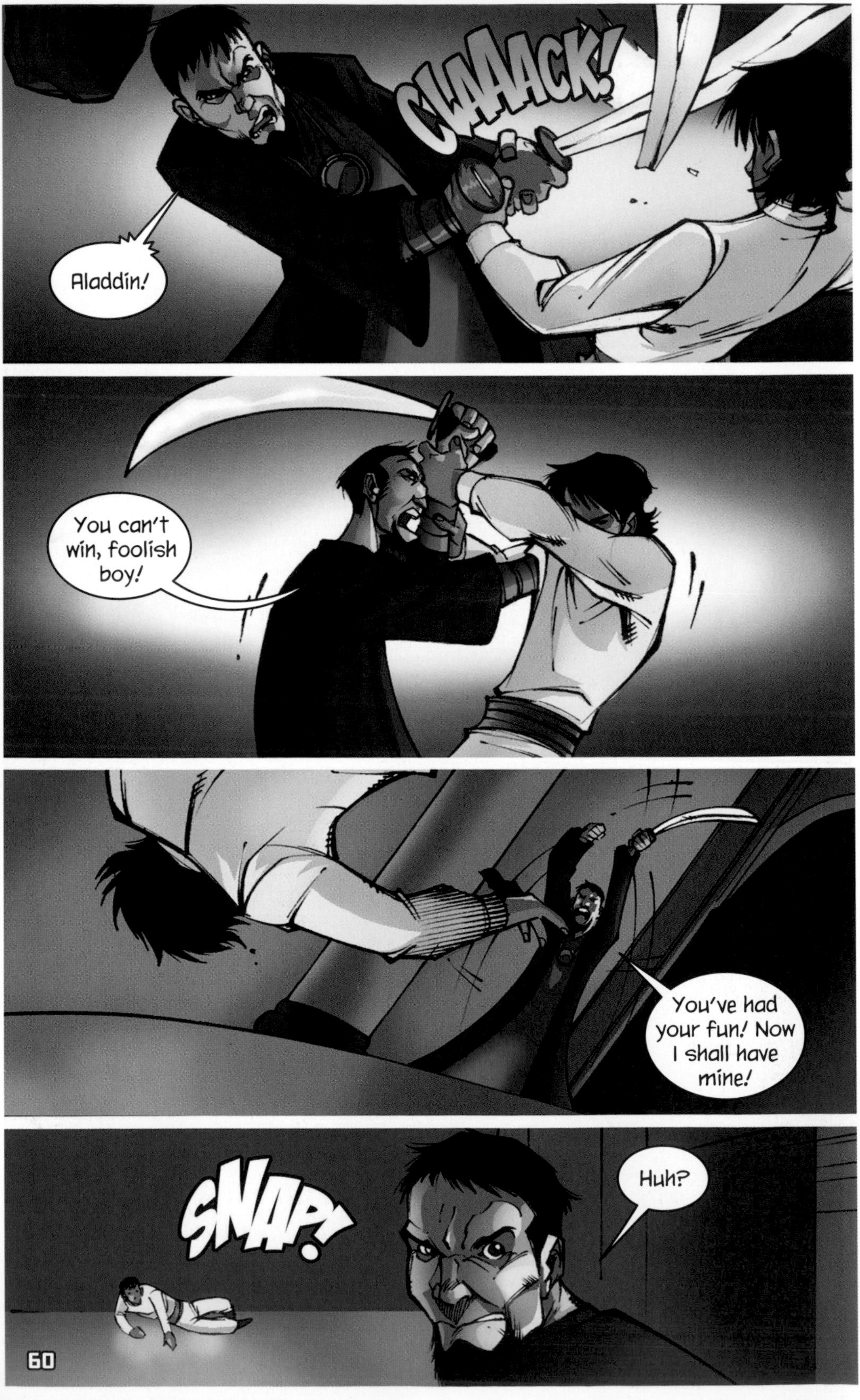
CLAAACK!
Aladdin!
You can't win, foolish boy!
You've had your fun! Now I shall have mine!
SNAP!
Huh?

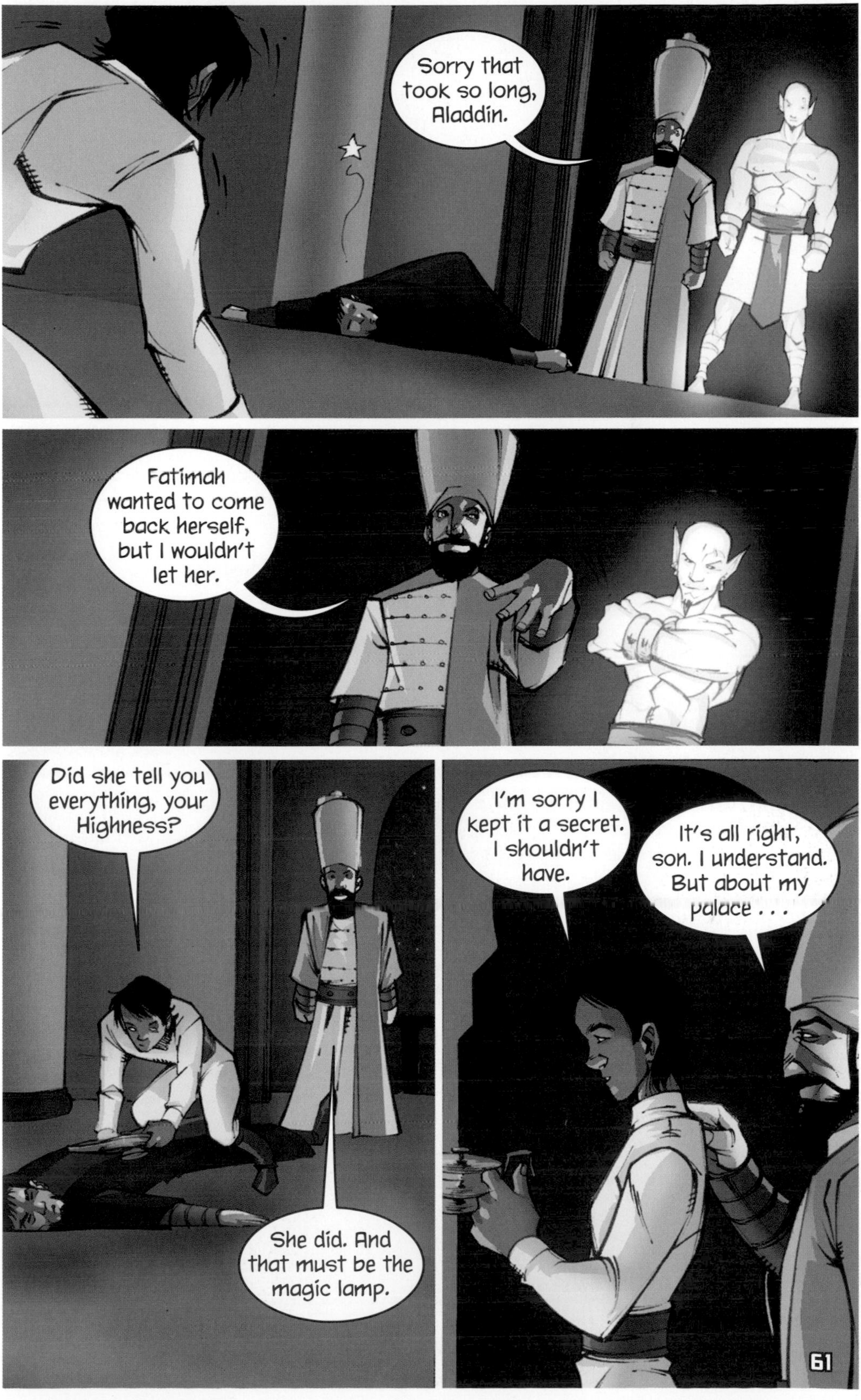
Sorry that took so long, Aladdin.
Fatimah wanted to come back herself, but I wouldn't let her.
Did she tell you everything, your Highness?
She did. And that must be the magic lamp.
I'm sorry I kept it a secret. I shouldn't have.
It's all right, son. I understand. But about my palace . . .

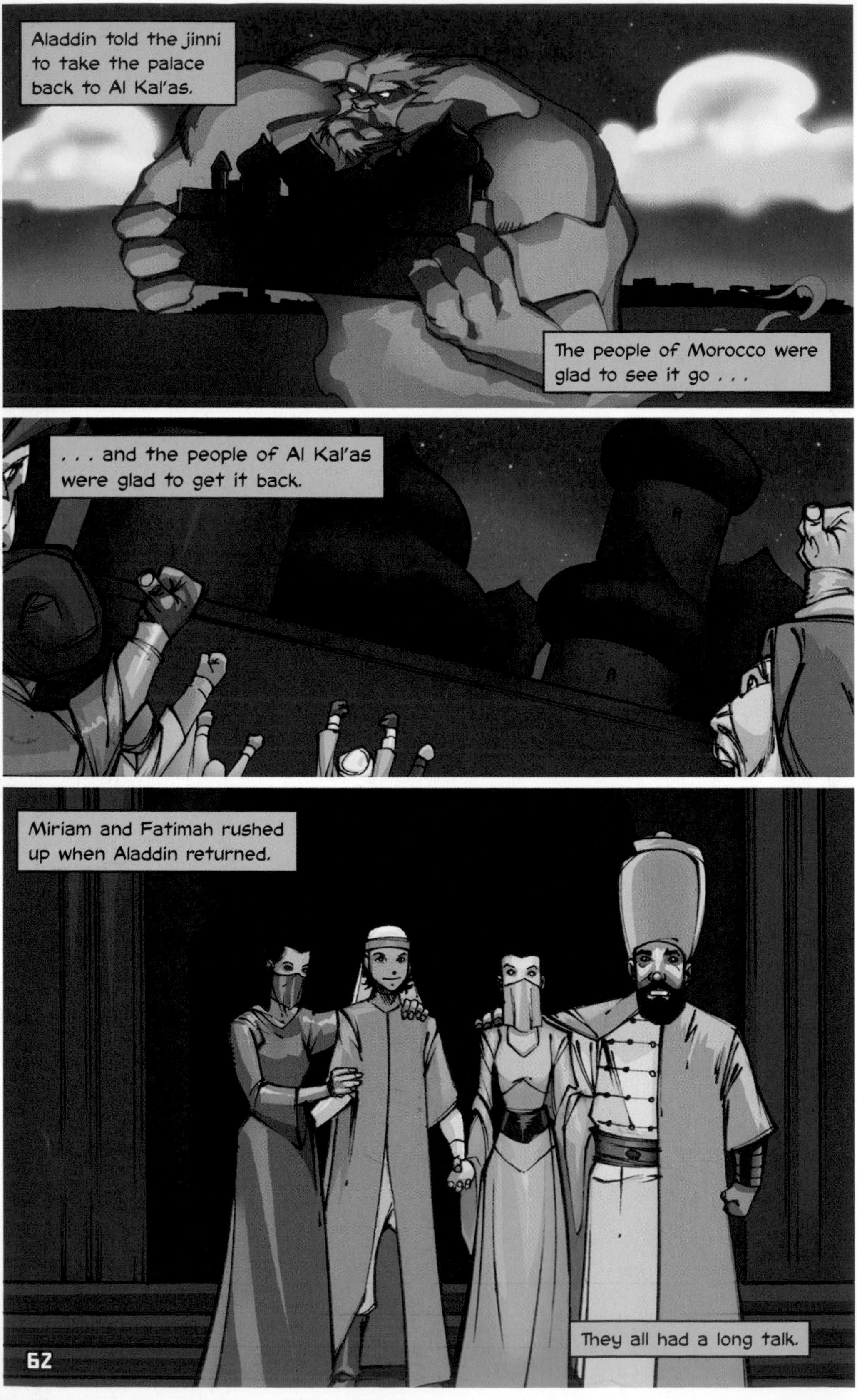
Aladdin told the jinni to take the palace back to Al Kal'as.
The people of Morocco were glad to see it go . . .
. . . and the people of Al Kal'as were glad to get it back.
Miriam and Fatimah rushed up when Aladdin returned.
They all had a long talk.

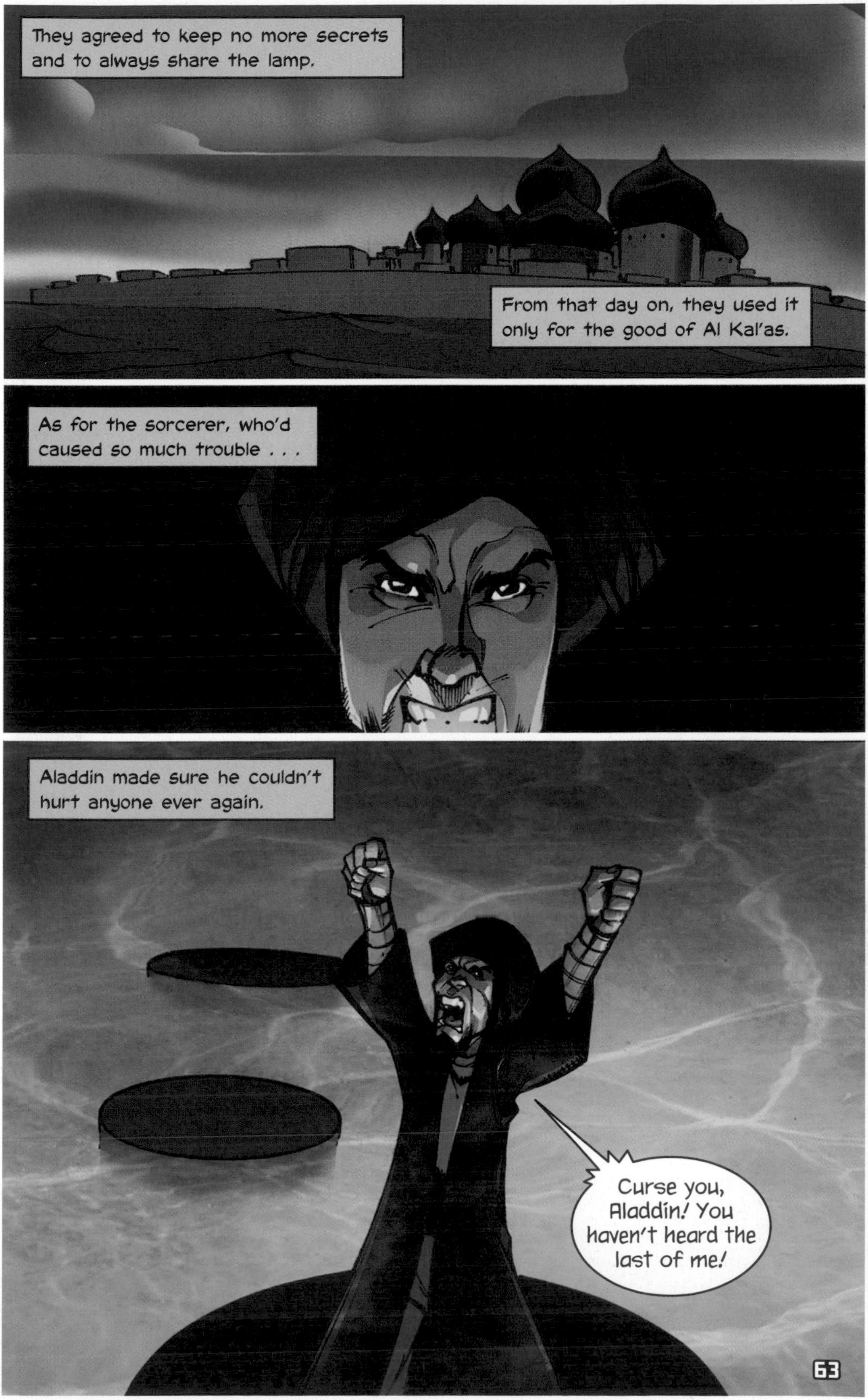
They agreed to keep no more secrets and to always share the lamp.
From that day on, they used it only for the good of Al Kal'as.
As for the sorcerer, who'd caused so much trouble . . .
Aladdin made sure he couldn't hurt anyone ever again.
Curse you, Aladdin! You haven't heard the last of me!

NIGHTS

The story of "Aladdin and the Magic Lamp" is part of a collection of Middle Eastern and South Asian folktales known as *One Thousand and One Nights*. These tales have been passed down from generation to generation for hundreds of years. The first English-language edition, titled *The Arabian Nights' Entertainment*, was published in 1706.

Since then, many versions of the book have been published — some containing more than 1,000 stories. In each of these editions, the tales of mystery and adventure are told by the same narrator, a beautiful woman named Scheherazade. She has just married an evil ruler who plans to kill her before the night is through. To stop him, Scheherazade entertains the king with a new story each night, and he soon forgets about his deadly plan.

The Arabian Nights tales remain some of the greatest stories ever told. They include popular adventures, such as "The Fisherman and the Genie," "the Seven Voyages of Sinbad," and "Ali Baba and the Forty Thieves." Many of these stories have been adapted into movies, books, and plays, which are still popular today.

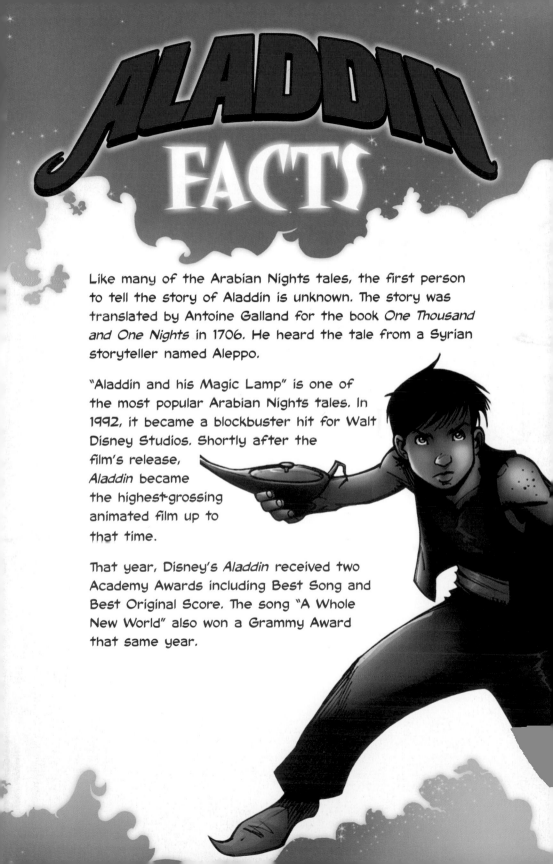

ALADDIN FACTS

Like many of the Arabian Nights tales, the first person to tell the story of Aladdin is unknown. The story was translated by Antoine Galland for the book *One Thousand and One Nights* in 1706. He heard the tale from a Syrian storyteller named Aleppo.

"Aladdin and his Magic Lamp" is one of the most popular Arabian Nights tales. In 1992, it became a blockbuster hit for Walt Disney Studios. Shortly after the film's release, *Aladdin* became the highest-grossing animated film up to that time.

That year, Disney's *Aladdin* received two Academy Awards including Best Song and Best Original Score. The song "A Whole New World" also won a Grammy Award that same year.

ABOUT THE AUTHOR

Carl Bowen is a writer and editor who lives in Lawrenceville, Georgia. He was born in Louisiana, lived briefly in England and was raised in Georgia where he attended grammar school, high school, and college. He has published a handful of novels and more than a dozen short stories, all while working at White Wolf Publishing as an editor and advertising copywriter. His first graphic novel, published by Udon Entertainment, is called *Exalted*.

ABOUT THE ILLUSTRATOR

Alfonso Ruiz was born in 1975 in Macuspana, Tabasco, in Mexico, where the temperature is just as hot as the sauce is. He became a comic book illustrator when he was 17 years old and has worked on many graphic novels since then. Alfonso has illustrated several English graphic novels, including retellings of *Dracula* and *Pinocchio*.

GLOSSARY

ashamed *(uh-SHAMED)*—a feeling of embarrassment or guilt

canopy *(KAN-uh-pee)*—a piece of cloth or other material often covering a bed

cavern *(KAV-ern)*—a large cave

ifrit *(EE-freet)*—a powerful, supernatural creature often found in Arabic and Islamic folktales

jinni *(JEE-nee)*—a magic spirit that serves the person who calls it

market *(MAR-kit)*—a place where people buy and sell food and goods

merchant *(MUR-chuhnt)*—someone who sells goods for profit

Morocco *(ma-RAH-koh)*—a country in northwest Africa, bordering the Atlantic Ocean and the Mediterranean Sea

oasis *(oh-AY-sis)*—a place in the desert where there is water and plants and trees

sorcerer *(SOR-sur-er)*—someone who performs magic by controlling evil spirits, often referred to as a wizard

sultan *(SUHLT-uhn)*—an emperor or ruler of some Muslim countries

vendor *(VEN-dur)*—a person who sells something

wage *(WAJE)*—the money someone is paid for his or her work

DISCUSSION QUESTIONS

1. The jinni can fulfill any wish. If you had a magic lamp, what three things would you ask for?

2. Aladdin didn't tell Princess Fatimah about the magic lamp. Why do you think he made this decision? Is it ever okay to withhold the truth from someone? Explain.

3. At the end of the story, the evil sorcerer promises to seek revenge against Aladdin. Do you think Aladdin will have to face him again? Why or why not?

WRITING PROMPTS

1. If you had a magic ring that could take you anywhere in the world, where would you go? Describe the place, and then write a story about your adventure there.

2. Do you think Aladdin and Princess Fatimah will live happily ever after? Write another chapter to this book. What adventures will they have next? Will they ever use the magic lamp again?

3. Imagine your own Arabian Nights tale. Think of a story filled with mystery and adventure. Then write it down and read it to friends and family.

STONE ARCH BOOKS

ALADDIN
and the
Magic
Lamp
GRAPHIC NOVEL
ADVENTURE
BOWEN · RUIZ

ALADDIN AND THE MAGIC LAMP

The legendary tale of Aladdin, a poor youth living in the city of Al Kal'as. One day, the crafty boy outsmarts an evil sorcerer, getting his hands on a magical lamp that houses a wish-fulfilling genie! Soon, all of Aladdin's dreams come true, and he finds himself married to a beautiful princess. All is well until, one day, the evil sorcerer returns to reclaim the lamp.

MANNING
OSNAYA
ALI BABA
AND THE FORTY THIEVES
GRAPHIC NOVEL
ADVENTURE

ALI BABA AND THE FORTY THIEVES

The legendary tale of Ali Baba, a young Persian boy who discovers a cave filled with gold and jewels, the hidden treasures of forty deadly thieves. Unfortunately, his greedy brother, Kasim, cannot wait to get his hands on the riches. Returning to the cave, he is captured by the thieves and killed, and now the evil men want revenge on Ali Baba as well.

ARABIAN NIGHTS TALES

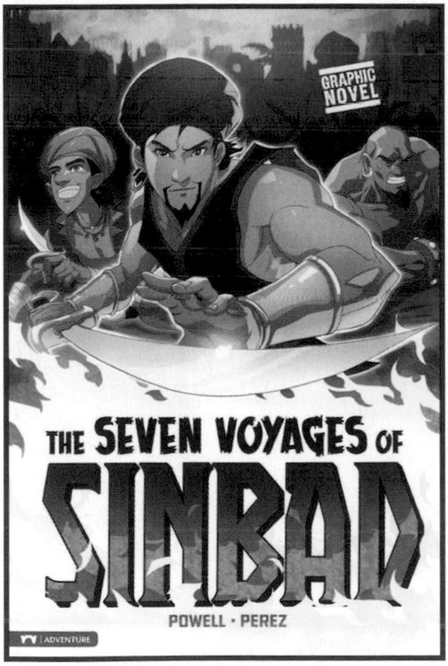
GRAPHIC NOVEL
THE SEVEN VOYAGES OF SINBAD
POWELL · PEREZ
ADVENTURE

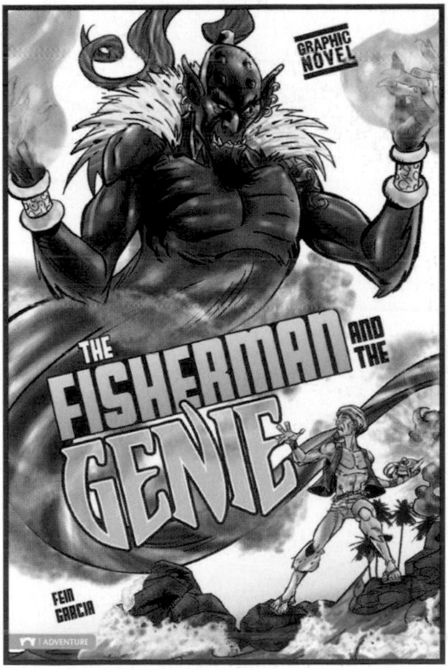
GRAPHIC NOVEL
THE FISHERMAN AND THE GENIE
FEIN GARCIA
ADVENTURE

THE SEVEN VOYAGES OF SINBAD

The tale of Sinbad the Sailor, who goes to sea in search of great riches and discovers even greater adventures. On his seven treacherous voyages, the Persian explorer braves a shipwreck, fights off savage cannibals, and battles a giant Cyclops, hoping to survive and tell his legendary story.

THE FISHERMAN AND THE GENIE

The legendary tale of an evil Persian king, who marries a new wife each day and then kills her the next morning. To stop this murderous ruler, a brave woman named Scheherazade risks her own life and marries the king herself . . . but not without a plan. On their wedding night, she will entertain him with the tale of the Fisherman and the Genie — a story so amazing, he'll never want it to end.

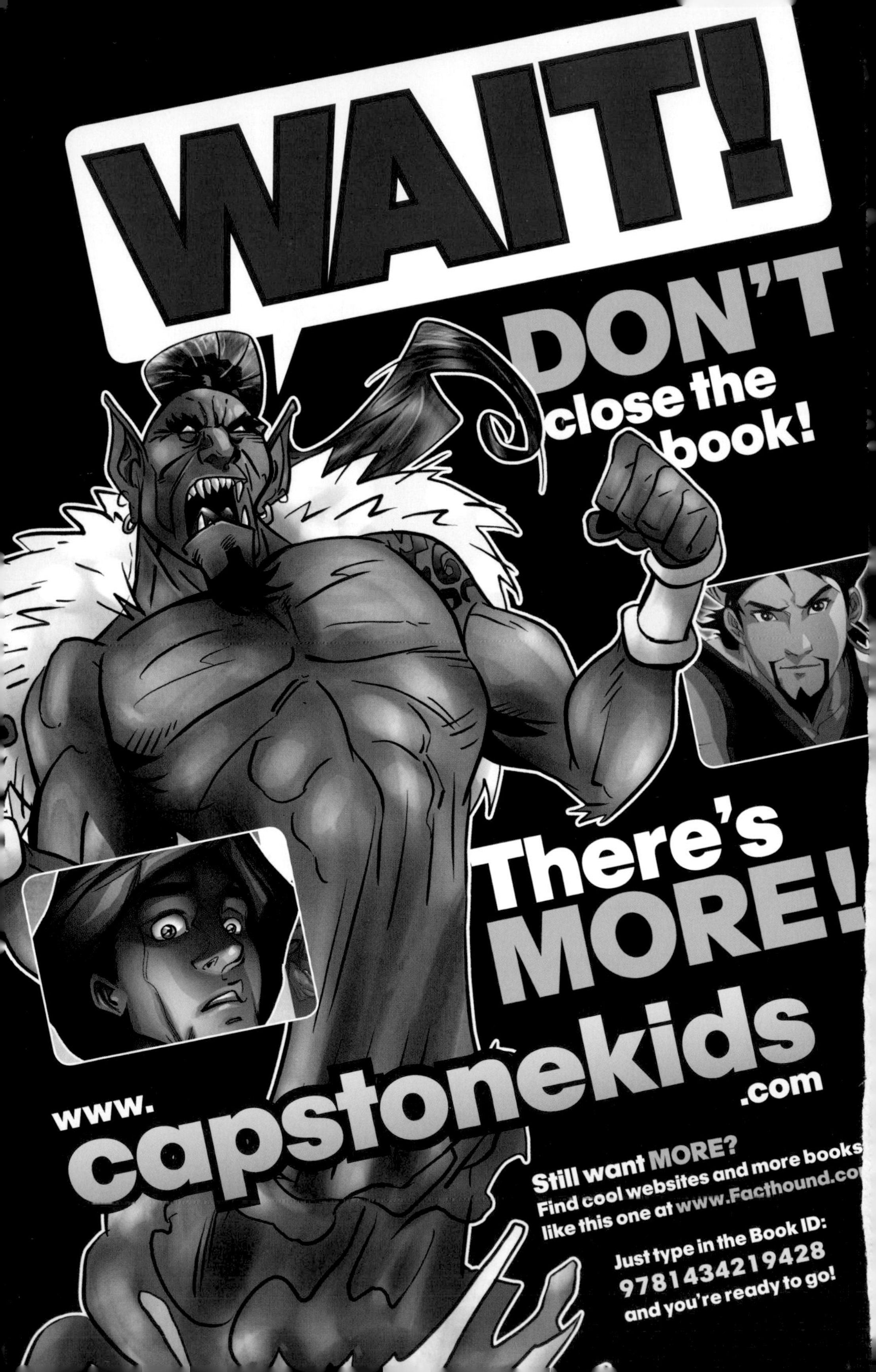

WAIT!
DON'T close the book!
There's MORE!
www. capstonekids .com
Still want MORE?
Find cool websites and more books
like this one at www.Facthound.co
Just type in the Book ID:
9781434219428
and you're ready to go!